'You're a good dancer,' she complimented him.

'I told you, I was taught by my head-hunting friends.' He went on, 'Who is the young man who looks as if he wants to hunt *my* head?'

'That's Will Roberts. He wants to be an anaesthetist.'

'Ah. So I can have my head hunted painlessly. Has he a proprietorial interest in you?'

She discovered she didn't want to tell Mark that Will was her boyfriend. 'He brought me here.'

'I see. Then the calmness of old age must give way to the impetuosity of youth. At the end of this you may rejoin him and I will go and eat.'

'I'm glad you've come to my party, and you're not old.'

'Ten years older than you, my dear.'

Gill Sanderson is a psychologist who finds time to write only by staying up late at night. Weekends are filled by her hobbies of gardening, running and mountain walking. Her ideas come from her work, from one son who is an oncologist, one son who is a nurse and her daughter who is a trainee midwife. She first wrote articles for learned journals and chapters for a textbook. Then she was encouraged to change to fiction by her husband, who is an established writer of war stories.

Recent titles by the same author:

A FAMILY TO SHARE*
A FAMILY AGAIN*

*Loving Sisters trilogy

A FAMILY FRIEND

BY
GILL SANDERSON

MILLS & BOON®

First published in Great Britain 1998
Harlequin Mills & Boon Limited,
Eton House, 18-24 Paradise Road, Richmond, Surrey TW9 1SR

© Gill Sanderson 1998

ISBN 0 263 81246 4

Set in Times Roman 10½ on 12 pt.
03-9811-49172-D

Printed and bound in Norway
by AiT Trondheim AS, Trondheim

CHAPTER ONE

Usually, Rosalind Grey didn't show her emotions, but when the rising sun first flashed across the sea she couldn't resist a gasp of delight. The tiny Pacific island which was their destination looked like an emerald on a plate of gold.

She turned her head. The government ship that had dropped them was now just a dark mark on the horizon. They were alone— just one small boat, buzzing across the water, and the island. She wondered what she'd find there.

'It's beautiful,' she said to Noah, the male nurse, who was piloting the little craft with all his ancestors' skill.

Noah beamed at her. 'Of course it is, missy,' he said, 'apart from the malaria, leprosy, beri-beri and dental caries.'

She laughed. 'You're a cynic, Noah. Spent too much time training in civilisation.'

'Where there's traffic accidents and pollution, as well as the other things. No, I like it here best.'

She pulled at her life-jacket and eased herself around, taking care not to rock the little boat. 'You visit this island every six months? Why, if there's a doctor there already?'

He shrugged. 'He'll only be here for a year. I need to come regularly—get to know people. But for a while they're lucky to have their own doctor. The next three islands have to manage with my odd visits and the radio if there's a real emergency.'

'I see.' For a while Rosalind was content just to sit. Seldom in her life had she seen such unspoiled beauty. But the mood soon passed. She was here to learn, perhaps to help. 'I'm glad Dr Parang gave me the chance to come with you,' she said. She smiled to herself. 'He wasn't very keen.'

She closed her eyes, remembering her first interview with Dr Parang, the head of the hospital that serviced this scattering of tiny Pacific islands. He hadn't been quite sure what to make of her. He'd rarely had the chance to welcome visitors from his old English medical school but... He'd looked at the small but formidable figure in front of him.

'The previous trainees have all been male,' he said doubtfully. 'Medicine here requires a certain toughness. But I'm sure we'll find something to interest you.'

'I feel I can do everything that my predecessors did,' Rosalind said frostily. 'Except perhaps play, or talk about, rugby. I certainly don't want an easy life.'

Dr Parang winced. He'd played rugby for the medical school. He had been rather looking forward to a chat about the respective England and Australian teams.

'I know you're supposed to just observe,' he said, 'but we are short-staffed. If you can help with treatment we'd be grateful.'

'I'm happy to do anything so long as there's someone in authority, such as yourself, that I can refer to. I'm here to work.'

Dr Parang appeared gratified. 'Most kind. We'll start you on the gynaecological ward,' he said, 'then perhaps the children's ward.'

'Work suitable for women?' Rosalind asked, still with ice in her voice.

Dr Parang smiled; she realised that for the first time he was feeling that he was scoring a point. 'I can assure you that you will find much of interest in the wards,' he murmured.

And she had. Medicine was practised in wards with walls open to the sea breeze. There were too many sick people and not enough equipment, not enough drugs, not enough skilled help. She 'observed' for half a day. In the afternoon she suggested what she could do, and was given her own patients.

Dr Parang watched and was impressed. He didn't need to supervise much. After a while he moved her to the medical and surgical wards. She watched, practised and learned. Without complaint she worked the ludicrously long hours. Perhaps she couldn't talk about rugby—but the doctor knew she was making his task easier.

Then she asked if she could go on one of the trips to the outlying islands.

Dr Parang frowned. 'I know you don't want a holiday,' he said, 'but these trips can be hard. Much of the time you'll travel by motorised canoe. Sleeping accommodation can be simple, if not downright uncomfortable.'

'I'd still like to go if I won't do any actual harm,' she said. 'I feel I've managed here quite well. Have you any complaints about my work?'

'Indeed, no. It has been…exemplary.' Like so many men before him, Dr Parang had learned that arguing with Rosalind was unproductive. It wasn't that she got angry or raised her voice, just that she always seemed to be right.

'You may go,' he said. 'There is much you will learn. I'm sure you'll cope—after all, you've coped with everything so far. And on Malapa Island you'll find one of your compatriots. He might be glad of a visit.' Dr Parang appeared to consider. 'There, again, he might not. I'll radio him, saying a trainee will be calling with Noah, but I'll not tell him which sex.'

This intrigued Rosalind but, having got her own way about the trip, she decided not to push her luck by demanding details.

For two days she'd travelled on the little government steamer, eating with Noah, the captain and crew and sleeping in a corner of the deck. Then, before dawn, she'd been dropped in the middle of the dark Pacific in a tiny boat loaded with medical supplies. It would be unsafe for the steamer to try to get closer. 'You'll enjoy the trip,' the captain said.

Rosalind thought of sharks and other less defined marine horrors. She nodded curtly. 'Of course I will.' She intended to.

Now, half an hour later, she knew the captain had been right. The island was getting nearer—she could make out individual palm trees. She could see light waves, breaking on the reef that surrounded the island. Expertly, Noah steered through a gap and into the calmer waters of the lagoon. 'Soon be there now, Miss Rosalind.'

The sea had turned from gold into an incredible blue, and the pre-dawn chill was disappearing. Soon, she knew, it would be stickily hot. On the sandy white beach ahead she could see naked little children, splashing and waving. Then the first adult appeared, a man dressed simply in a brightly coloured pareu—the wrap-around skirt worn by both sexes. Other men and women followed. The entire village must have turned out to greet them.

Behind her Noah said in a surprised voice, 'No Dr Mark on shore. I would have thought he'd come down…'

'Perhaps he's busy,' Rosalind suggested.

'Perhaps he is.' Noah was not convinced.

The little boat touched the sand. Before she could step out a dozen men had splashed into the water, grabbed the gunwales and hauled the boat and its passengers well onto the beach. She was aware of the amazed, wide eyes of the children and the rapid chatter of the adults.

Pulling up her pareu, she stepped stiffly out of the boat. Then she unbuckled her life-jacket. It was already too hot inside it.

Noah issued orders and the boxes and bags in the boat were lifted out and carried up the beach. Something was wrong—he looked troubled. Now, she noticed, the men and women speaking to him did not have the usual big smiles she'd come to expect.

'Dr Mark doesn't come because he's ill,' Noah translated. 'He's sick, he can't get out of bed. But why hasn't he radioed for help?'

'Let's go to find out,' she said.

She followed Noah's reassuringly solid form as they walked first through the mangrove swamp and then into a grove of coconut trees. It was hot out of the breeze, and she felt the first trickle of sweat down her back. She was dressed as everyone here was—in a cotton T-shirt and pareu—but still she felt the heat. She would have liked to have gone barefoot, but had quickly learned that injuries and infections of the feet thrived here.

The procession passed through the little village—a dozen men with bags and packages on their heads, Noah and Rosalind, and a crowd of onlookers, following behind. She'd now got used to being a source of good-humoured curiosity. A quarter of a mile beyond the village they came to the doctor's house.

It was built on a little knoll to take advantage of what breeze there might be. Like the native huts, it was built of wood with a corrugated-iron roof. Unlike the native huts, it was very, very neat. There was an almost military precision about the shell path, the garden, the single table and chair on the verandah and the mosquito nets in the open windows. In the background she could hear the ever-present rattle of the diesel generator, powering the electrical supply.

Noah ordered the boxes—and Rosalind's own tiny bag—to be stored in an outhouse. Then he spoke again and the villagers reluctantly moved away.

'They are worried,' Noah said, 'but I have told them I will speak to them later.'

He led the way across the verandah and tapped on the side of the doorway. An anxious-looking girl, aged about eighteen, came quickly to let them in. There was another swift exchange in the native tongue, then the girl turned to Rosalind and said carefully, 'Good morning, Miss Rosalind. I am pleased to meet you.'

'The doctor is teaching Matilda to speak English,' Noah explained.

They stepped straight into the main room. It seemed to double as surgery and living room and was totally bare of any personal touch. In a corner were chairs and a table. There was a cane couch, a rack of books and the usual radio—nothing to suggest the character of the resident except the implacable neatness.

'Matilda says the doctor has recently got worse,' Noah said, after another swift conversation. 'He became ill very quickly.' He opened a door at the back of the living room. 'Dr Mark, it's Noah,' he called. There was no reply. He and Rosalind entered the room.

The bedroom was equally neat and spare. There was a wardrobe, a chest of drawers and a pile of boxes, but Rosalind's eyes were drawn to the still figure on the narrow bed.

He was lying on his front, one arm on the floor. She could see a shock of dark blond hair and a beard. The sheet that covered the man was damp but he was shivering and his breathing was laboured, stertorous.

'Doctor needs a doctor,' Noah said anxiously.

'Yes,' she said. 'Pity I'm not one—yet.'

She remembered the words of her lecturer. 'First, ABC. Check airway, breathing, circulation. Then don't be in too much of a hurry with your diagnosis. Always ask as much as possible, before examining or treating. Find out what happened.' She turned to Noah.

After another swift conversation with Matilda Noah said, 'Two days ago there was a big wind. Dr Mark was in one of the huts when the roof fell in. A piece of metal roof dropped on him and his back was gashed bad. He told Matilda here to clean the cut and to dress it. She did, but next day the doctor didn't get out of bed.'

Rosalind looked at Matilda's desperate face and leaned over to pat the girl's arm. 'I'm sure you did everything you could,' she said gently. 'Now, let's have a look.'

She knelt by the bed. The man looked to be in his early thirties. She could see pain lines around his eyes and mouth. 'Dr Harrison,' she said, 'can you hear me? I'm Rosalind Grey.'

An eye opened in the pain-racked face, surprisingly blue against the tanned skin and dark blond hair. For a lightning moment she was reminded of the morning sea after the golden glow of dawn.

For a while his expression was vague, then she saw him make an effort and intelligence returned, although he didn't raise his head. 'What are you doing here?' he muttered.

'I'm a trainee medical student. I'm here on my elective.'

Even through the pain she could see his surprise. 'Medical student? But you're a—'

'Please don't say I'm a woman,' she said peevishly. 'I already know.'

'I'm sure you do. Well, woman trainee doctor, you're on your own. You could radio for another doctor but it would be two or three days before anyone arrived. You'll just have to do the best you can yourself. Good luck.' He sighed, his eyes closed and he lapsed into unconsciousness.

His voice had been soft and weak, but there had been a definite sardonic overtone that she found unsettling. He doesn't seem worried about his predicament, she thought to herself. But I am.

On the chest of drawers was a stout canvas bag— she'd seen the other island doctors with one. Inside were the tools of their trade. She took out what she needed and gave him a quick examination. His pulse was fast and thready. His temperature was far too high—she could tell that by putting her hand on his forehead. But he was shivering. She didn't think the profuse sweating was caused by the heat. When she looked at his fingernails she could see signs of cyanosis. But it was his blood pressure that was the cause for real concern. It was far, far too low.

It was time to look at the injury. Pulling back the sheet, she uncovered a wound—a deep cut in his shoulder. Her mouth twisted. It was the one place on the body that a person could neither examine closely nor treat. The wound had been cleaned and dressed, and clumsily applied plastic butterfly stitches held it closed.

Gently she felt the side of the cut. Beneath her, the semiconscious man gasped with pain. Rosalind winced. She thought there was something still in the cut. It would have to come out.

Once again, as taught, she reviewed all the information she had. No matter how busy you are, the lecturer had said, don't make an instantaneous decision. Ninety-nine per cent of the time you will be right. One per cent might be wrong. Think a minute. So she thought. In the past she had made more difficult diagnoses than this but this time she was alone, with was no superior to help her.

'I think it's septicaemia,' she said. 'What used to be called blood poisoning. And it's led to septic shock. It's not so common now we have antibiotics but—'

'Infection can take hold quicker out here where it's hot and damp,' Noah said. 'Lot of Western doctors are surprised.'

She nodded. Although she'd read about it, it was still a shock to see how quickly infection could spread out here in the tropics. 'We'll set up an IV line and get some fluid into him,' she said decisively. 'And he needs a massive dose of antibiotics. I wonder if he's taken any already?'

While Noah questioned Matilda, Rosalind quickly scanned the surfaces in the bedroom. She was sure such a neat person would have his drugs handy but there was no sign of any. 'Matilda says he took no drugs,' Noah reported.

She still needed to be sure. Knowing that she would cause him pain, she shook the sleeping man and watched him force himself back to consciousness. The pain-filled blue eyes twitched open again and focussed on her blearily.

'Dr Harrison, I need to know. Did you take any antibiotics?'

She could see the effort it took to think about the question and the torment it took to answer. 'No,' he gasped. 'Guess I left it a bit late.'

'I thought I'd give you...' she said, but it was too late. He'd lapsed into unconsciousness.

The decision would have to be hers.

She left Noah to erect the IV line and Matilda found her the key and took her to the drug store. It was an antique fridge-freezer, powered by the diesel generator. Rosalind looked at his stock. pursed her lips and made her choice. He needed a big dose as he was a big man. And she thought he needed it urgently. She chose ampicillin, a broad-based antibiotic. She'd just have to hope he didn't have an allergic reaction to it.

Noah had set up the IV line and she added the antibiotic to the fluid dripping into his body.

'We'll wait a couple of hours and I hope he'll stabilise a little,' she said to Noah, 'but I'm not very happy about that cut on his back. I want to open it again and clean it. I think there might be something dirty still inside.'

'Yes, Miss Rosalind,' Noah said gravely. 'That seems good to me. Now, shall I ask Matilda to get us some breakfast?'

She realised that she'd had a long morning—and an eventful one! Glancing at her watch, she saw that it was only ten o'clock. 'I think I need some breakfast,' she said. 'This is turning out to be a full day.'

Breakfast was simple but satisfying—fruit, coffee with powdered milk and the local bread but, of course, no butter. However, with the bread was tinned marmalade. Rosalind hadn't felt the slightest twinge of homesickness since she'd arrived but the taste of marmalade made her think of her sisters, of the cheerful camaraderie of her fellow medical students and of the breakfasts they'd shared in the hospital canteen. Of the help she'd always been able to ask for.

You're just confusing the issue, she told herself. In hospital in England you'd deal with this easily.

After breakfast she felt more confident. She searched through Dr Harrison's medical supplies, looking for what she needed. It was easy to find. He appeared to be almost obsessively neat—everything was recorded and itemised. She found a large ledger with weekly results, apparently an analysis of blood specimens, carefully tabulated. There was also a set of charts that appeared to set out the relationships between a set of people—the natives on the island she guessed. She shut the book at once as this was not her business, then went to look again at the man she had now decided was her patient.

His hair was long and he had a beard. On the whole,

she didn't like men with beards. She thought they might be trying to hide something.

How could she judge character from the face of an ill, sleeping man? She didn't think this man looked to be an obsessive. It was an interesting face. There were pain lines on it, etched by experience and not smoothed away by sleep. It was not the face of a man concerned only with detail. Was it the face of a man needing something to occupy his mind? She didn't know.

'What is Dr Harrison doing on this island, Noah?' she asked.

Noah shrugged. 'He could have stayed on many islands. I know Dr Panang wanted him to stay and work at the hospital but Dr Harrison says he has research to do. So this island alone has its own doctor.'

'I see,' said Rosalind, though she didn't.

She checked the recumbent figure, then turned to the phials and carefully sealed instruments she was going to need. 'We need to do this minor operation together,' she said to Noah.

He nodded. 'I've helped before,' he said. 'I'll lay out the tray and scrub up.'

First was the local anaesthetic. She injected around the affected area with lignocaine then waited for it to take effect. As she waited she had time to look at the muscular back below her. The man was lean, no fat on the body at all. Any less fat and he'd have been emaciated, but there was the swell of back muscles. This was a man who was more than fit—he was strong.

Using tweezers, she carefully pulled off the butterfly stitches and tossed them into a dish. The wound didn't look good. 'I'm going to have to probe,' she told Noah, 'There's something in that wound.' As she picked up a scalpel she saw him lick his lips. He's worried that I can't do it, she guessed, and a mirthless smile creased her lips. She knew she could.

The wound bled, of course, but Noah swabbed at her command, and at the bottom of the gash she found what she'd suspected— rusty slivers of iron. There was no telling what was on them, but patiently she eased them out and then irrigated the wound.

The gash had gone deep into the muscle but she wasn't going to close it. Instead she sprayed some of the ampicillin onto sterile gauze and packed the wound with it. This would keep the wound open and ensure that it granulated from the bottom outwards. No infection would be sealed in. Finally Noah placed a thick, loose dressing on top.

'We've done a good job,' she told her nurse as they stripped off their rubber gloves. 'I'd have liked to give him oxygen, but we have none.'

'Good to work with you, Miss Rosalind,' Noah said. 'I hope Doctor knows what you've done for him.'

'He'll know when he wakes up with that shoulder,' she said practically, 'but I guess the fever will still have him. He's not out of the woods yet.'

There was nothing more she could do now but wait and hope the antibiotic would take effect. Her patient appeared fit and strong and should pull through, but still this was the first time she'd ever taken complete responsibility for a case. Stop worrying, she told herself. You know you've done everything according to the book.

When she and Noah eventually walked out of the bedroom she glanced at her watch. It was only midday! She felt as if she'd been working for ever. So much had happened.

'I have to set up my clinic for tomorrow,' Noah told her. 'There's nothing you can do to help and nothing much for you to see. Why don't you stay here with Matilda and keep an eye on the doctor? Perhaps you should get some rest, too. You started the day early.'

'So did you,' she flashed back.

Noah grinned. 'I could certainly do with some help tomorrow,' he said. 'I doubt if the doctor will be much use. You'd be fresher if you rested today.'

What he said made sense. 'All right,' she said, 'but, remember, I do anything you'd ask a male trainee to do.'

'I'll remember, miss. Now, Matilda!'

Matilda showed her into one of the two guest bedrooms. The tiny room was simple but clean. Rosalind dropped her bag, then went for a shower. Suddenly she felt tired—reaction, she guessed. And for two days on the steamer she'd had to wash in salt water. It was good to rinse the stickiness away.

She felt better afterwards and decided not to sleep. Instead, she accepted a drink from Matilda and looked in on the doctor again. He was still feverish and his pulse still thready, but she thought there was a tiny improvement in his condition.

When she'd first examined him she'd jotted down her findings on a handy scrap of paper. It had been drummed into her to write down *every* observation. Now she sat in the bedroom, took a fresh sheet of paper and carefully copied everything she'd noted. If another doctor took over this case he'd find it well documented.

She sat for a moment, then went back to her room and fetched a leather-bound book. She'd kept a journal since she was a child, writing in it not regularly but when she felt she had something to say. Since coming to the Pacific she'd had something to write practically every day.

'Not even a doctor and got my first case,' she wrote. 'Sea miles from anywhere and the one person who is ill is the doctor.' Then she noted her observations, her conclusions and what she had done. At the end of her medical account she wrote, 'Obviously not had a chance to talk to him yet. He's got too much hair. A beard! But his eyes are a glorious blue and he seems a nice person.' Then she blushed.

Matilda had brought a cane chair into the bedroom so she could sit by her patient. After putting down her journal, she decided she'd sit by him in case there was any change.

The afternoon got gently hotter and outside the leaves rustled in the sea breeze. Her cane chair was comfortable so she thought she'd close her eyes just for a moment. Her head fell back and she slept.

Rosalind was annoyed when she woke. Doctors didn't sleep on duty! She was more annoyed when she looked at her watch—she'd slept for two hours. There were good reasons, of course—lack of sleep on the steamer, her early start, the excitement of new landfall and then the discovery that she had to act as a doctor. But reasons weren't excuses. She couldn't forgive herself.

Her patient had woken her. He was restless, moaning. She steadied him with a hand on his shoulder and readjusted the IV line taped to his forearm. When she felt his forehead she thought his temperature was down a little more and certainly his pulse was stronger.

She leaned over the bed and tried to ease him back

into the centre. He was heavy! But she'd learned from the nursing staff how to handle patients who seemed immovable in bed.

He moaned again, and slowly his eyes opened as she pulled his pillow straight. She could see the doubt in them as he focussed on her. His eyes really were an incredible blue. They changed the rest of his face—made harsh by the beard—into something more friendly, more appealing. Suddenly he was no longer a case, a medical problem, but a person.

As sometimes happened in cases of fever, there was a sudden return of consciousness. Dr Mark Harrison knew who he was. What he didn't know was who *she* was.

'Good afternoon—or morning or evening. Who're you?' His voice was hoarse but she thought there was a warmth to it that she liked.

As she leaned back he tried to turn to look at her. 'Ow!' he grunted, and she saw the beads of perspiration spring out along his hairline. 'And what happened to my shoulder?'

He had rolled onto the injury. She had packed the dressing as thickly as possible but she knew it would still be very sore.

'I'm Rosalind Grey,' she said, 'and it's now afternoon. Your shoulder hurts because I opened the cut on it again. There were fragments in it—I thought I'd better cut them out.' She could see him trying to grapple with this bit of news. 'Hmm,' he said. 'I got Matilda to clean it up as best she could but it's hard to direct operations looking over your shoulder into a mirror. Yes, I guess I needed a doctor.'

She hoped he wasn't going to be awkward about this.

She didn't think he would be. 'Actually,' she said, 'I'm only a doctor in training. I'm in my fifth year, though. I'm here on my elective.' The elective was the period when all medical students took off for two months to see something of medical life in hospitals other than their own. Some just found another hospital but the lucky ones managed to find a hospital abroad.

'In training or not, I'm very grateful for what you did, Miss Rosalind Grey. I really am. I should have treated myself with more care. But sometimes...' His voice trailed away.

He was more alert now, looking at her assessingly but not unpleasantly. She was uncomfortably aware that her dress—a pareu printed with dancing palm trees and a white T shirt showing a sunset—was not one to inspire medical confidence. For a moment she longed for her short white coat with the stethoscope hanging out of the pocket.

He went on, 'But what is a—'

She interrupted him. 'I hope you're not going to ask why a little woman like me, so obviously young, has come to a wild and distant place like this?'

He blinked. 'Do you read minds as well as practise medicine? Yes, I was going to say something exactly like that. But now I'm sorry.'

It seemed a genuine apology and she warmed as he smiled at her. She decided to explain to him. 'My hospital trained Dr Parang who is in charge of the main island hospital here. When he first got the job he wrote to his old hospital, offering a place for a student doing their elective. Students have been coming for five years now.'

'So why did the hospital pick you?'

It was a fair question, and not asked challengingly. 'There was a competition and the prize was the fare here.'

'What kind of competition?' He was certainly persistent.

'We all had to submit a three-thousand-word essay on nuclear medicine and its future.'

'So, do you know a lot about nuclear medicine?'

'I know a lot more than when I started my research,' she said honestly.

'Could I read your essay some time? Do you have it with you?'

Well, no, she hadn't. She'd known that her packing had to be kept to the absolute minimum. 'I could post you a copy,' she offered, 'if you're really interested.'

'I am. I need to keep up with the latest developments in nuclear medicine out here.'

He was teasing her, of course, but for once she didn't mind. She was enjoying talking to him. However, his voice was weakening. He needed a doctor, not a friend. 'I think you should sleep some more,' she said. 'You've been really quite ill.'

'I know. Is there—' his voice was fading '—anything else I need to tell you?'

'Nothing at all. Try to relax, I can cope.'

Somehow his voice managed to be both sleepy and sardonic. 'I'll bet you always cope.' Then his eyes closed.

For a moment she stood, looking down at him, his naked body outlined by the thin sheet. A patient, she told herself, he's just a patient. Then she went in search of Matilda.

CHAPTER TWO

NEXT morning she and Noah discussed what to do. Noah was a trained nurse, of course, and the night before he had helped the comatose Mark to wash. Rosalind had told him that she'd sleep in the living room to be within earshot of the ill man, and he'd agreed to this. But there had been no need to worry. Each of the three times she'd slipped out of bed to check on him he'd been sleeping peacefully.

'I'd better do my work, Miss Rosalind,' Noah said. 'Usually the doctor helps me, but on the other islands I manage on my own so I can do so here. Perhaps you'd better stay with Dr Mark.'

'I came to help you,' she said.

He shrugged. 'If you weren't here then I'd have to look after the doctor. That would be a problem. You're helping me by stopping me worrying. And we've got another three islands to visit where you can watch and help.'

'If you're sure.' The last thing she wanted was to be given an easy life.

'It's not hard work today. Give out the vitamins, do the injections. On the other islands I have to decide if anyone is going to need a doctor and radio for one. Here, Dr Mark does all that.'

'I'll stay, then. Perhaps he'll wake up later.' She thought he was responding well to treatment. For breakfast he'd had a fruit drink and some unripe coconut juice and had promptly gone back to sleep.

He dozed all morning then woke properly at lunch-time. 'Just need to do my observations,' she said briskly, and he was largely silent as she tested blood pressure, pulse and temperature. 'You're a lot better,' she said, as she carefully filled in her results on the sheet she'd started for him. 'The fever is well down. How d'you feel?'

'Not happy,' he said morosely. 'I'm weak, which doesn't suit me. I feel a fool and my shoulder aches like fury.'

'I'm not surprised at the pain. It was a deep cut and I had to probe around in it. Would you like some kind of painkiller? There's paracetamol or you could have morphine if there is any.'

He tried to shrug, then winced. 'No, thanks. I'll live with the ache—it'll be a lesson to me. I mustn't think I'm immune from illness because I'm a doctor.'

'Every doctor should be ill at least once,' she told him. 'You sympathise more with the patient if you've been one. Being ill stops you getting complacent.'

'I promise I'll never be complacent again. When have you been ill, Dr Grey?'

'I told you, I'm not a doctor yet. And I'm afraid I've not been ill since I was a child.'

'So will you get complacent?'

Rosalind knew her own faults—and being too confi-dent in her own judgement was one of them. Yes, if she didn't take care she could get complacent. But no way was she going to tell that to this man.

'I try not to be,' she said. 'I think in medicine there's

a thin line between confidence and complacency. I try to stick to it. Anyway, like I said, I'm still a trainee.'

'You could have fooled me.' He grimaced as he pushed down on the bed. 'I want to sit up.'

She helped him, slipping an arm under his uninjured shoulder and easing him up the bed. The patients she. had dealt with in hospital had been clad in regulation nightdresses or pyjamas, and this man was naked. It was different, feeling the skin of his back against her bare arm. It was slightly unsettling.

She took refuge in sounding professional. 'Are you hungry?' she asked. 'Shall I ask Matilda to cook you something?'

He shook his head. 'I don't want to eat, I'll just have some more fruit juice. Perhaps some coffee later.'

'You should eat—you need to keep your strength up. And there's not a lot of fat on you.'

'You've noticed, then?' he asked.

She couldn't help looking at him again. He was leaning against the cane headboard of the bed, the sheet bunched round his hips. He was tanned—unusually so for a blond—and when he moved the muscles rippled under his golden skin. She blushed slightly, she didn't know why. She'd seen naked men before.

'Obviously we are taught to consider physique in any diagnosis,' she said stiffly. 'Your musculature is extremely good—comparable to that of a trained athlete. But highly trained athletes are more susceptible to illness.'

'You've got the right doctor's attitude,' he said with a grin. 'Kind but bossy.'

'I'm not bossy!' she said indignantly. He looked at her until she had to look away, embarrassed. 'Well, perhaps at times I do get a bit carried away.' She tried to change the subject. 'How is it that you are so fit?'

'I run six miles along the beach every morning. And every afternoon I swim for an hour in the lagoon. Not the last three days, of course.'

'Isn't that rather a lot?'

'I like it,' he said simply. 'It makes me feel good.'

This is an odd conversation, she thought to herself.

There was a brief pause, and then he said, 'If you don't mind asking Matilda, I'd like a drink. Pineapple juice would be great.'

'Of course, I'll ask her at once.' She'd been too engrossed in talking when she should have been attending to her patient. He had been ill and he was still weak. She opened the door and called. As ever, Matilda was working—but working well within earshot. She scurried off to fetch the drink.

'How's Noah doing?' Mark asked. 'I usually like to help him.'

'He says he can cope and you're not to worry. Why does he come here when you're here already?'

'He's the district nurse.' Mark grinned. 'It's just that his district is spreads over several hundred square miles. And I'm not really the doctor here, I'm doing some research.'

There was a timid knock on the door and in came Matilda with two glasses of juice on a tray. Mark took his and sipped. 'Thank you, Matilda,' he said, 'This fruit juice is delicious.'

Matilda looked delighted. With great care she said, 'I am pleased that you like it, Doctor. The fruit has been freshly picked this morning.'

'The fruit *was* freshly picked the morning,' he corrected her gently. 'Don't you think Matilda's English is good, Dr Grey?'

'I certainly do,' Rosalind said. In fact, she'd been thinking what a good teacher Mark was.

She noticed there was a paleness under his tan. Taking the glass from him, she said, 'You're looking tired again. Let me help you down the bed and you can sleep some more.'

'Doctor's orders,' he said.

On the following morning he said he felt much better, and told her she was to go out with Noah. She'd come here to observe, and she should do so.

'You're much better when the doctor says you are,' she replied as she wrote up her observations. 'But you're right—the fever is down and you should be all right with Matilda.'

She felt a certain reluctance to leave him, she wasn't quite sure why. Noah was taking her to the second, smaller village about two miles away. If anything went wrong a runner would soon fetch them back. And to watch Noah at work was why she had come. As she walked down the shell path and into the warm damp jungle she wished she was staying with Mark.

However, once at the village she enjoyed herself. She sat with Noah in a little hut made of bamboo and palm fronds. The sides were open, and the saltiness of the sea breeze combated the heaviness of the scents from the vegetation behind them.

It was surprising how many of the jobs of a district nurse in the Pacific were similar to the jobs of a district nurse in England. There were children to be injected, pregnant mothers to be given supplements. Noah had a variety of medicines for assorted illnesses, and bandages and dressings for cuts. And there was always advice to be given.

Watching him, Rosalind realised how much good could be done with the simplest of drugs. Hospital medicine with its complex machines and techniques was all very well, but Noah was saving lives with very little.

There were three cases Noah wasn't happy about. One old man had an ulcer on his leg which was not responding to the powder he'd been given. A child was limping—there appeared to be something wrong with his hip joint. Another man had an eye infection and Noah couldn't decide on the cause. Each person was told to report to the doctor—but not for a week.

'Dr Mark will either treat them or radio for help,' Noah told her with a huge smile. 'This saves me from making decisions. Costs a lot to have doctor come out here and find there's nothing much wrong.'

'He must be handy to have here,' she agreed. 'Why d'you think he—?'

She was interrupted by the sound of screaming from the far end of the village. Towards them rushed a bunch of anxious mothers, carrying a wailing form between them. They started to shout details as soon as they saw that Noah had seen them.

Noah listened. 'There's been an accident,' he said, and carefully handed the tiny baby he'd been holding on his knees back to her mother. 'Out in the coconut grove. I'll bet…'

He stepped to the doorway of the hut and took the shaking body of a small boy from the arms of the women carrying him. Rosalind leaned over and placed her hand on the blood-drenched pad one woman was holding to his head. A couple of stern commands in the native tongue and the women retreated from the doorway to gather some distance away, wailing and groaning.

Gently Noah laid the body on the white-cloth-covered boxes they were using as a table. The boy was about eight, dressed simply in a brief pareu. Blood ran from under the pad, down over his eyes and onto his thin bare chest.

Rosalind ripped open a sterile dressing, moved the pad and clamped the dressing in place. She caught a glimpse of a long gash across the temple, with some bruising in the middle.

'Skull wounds always bleed a lot,' Noah said calmly. 'We'll wait a while till the flow stops.'

'What happened?' Rosalind asked.

Noah smiled without humour. 'It's funny till it happens to you. A coconut fell on his head. They're heavy and they've got quite a distance to fall. There've been more than a few deaths from falling coconuts.'

'I'm wondering about concussion,' Rosalind said. 'His breathing is shallow and he looks pale.' With her spare hand she reached for the boy's wrist. 'Pulse is fast and weak.'

From a box Noah took a silver space blanket and spread it over the boy. 'We'll know more in a moment.'

If Rosalind had been working in an A and E department she would have asked for a head X-ray as a matter of course. But the nearest X-ray machine was hundreds of miles away. They'd have to do the best they could.

The boy seemed calmer now. While Rosalind kept her hand on the dressing Noah rolled back each eyelid. They both looked, then glanced at each other. Rosalind took a pocket light and flashed it into each eye in turn.

'Pupils react to light,' she said, 'and they're equal in size, not dilated.'

Noah nodded. 'I doubt he's concussed.'

'Just a very nasty gash where the bone is nearest the surface. It's going to take some demon stitching.'

'You can do it,' Noah said.

'But I'm still not a real doctor.'

Noah pointed at the now still child. 'He doesn't know that. All he wants is to get well. I'll take the responsibility, if you like. I saw you working on Dr Mark. You've got the fingers for this kind of thing and I know I couldn't do as well as that. You have sutured before?'

She had sutured before. Without being immodest, she knew she was good at it. 'If I do it I'll take the blame,' she said, 'but I think we'd better wait a while till he's calmer.'

Noah carried the boy into an adjoining hut, took a fresh dressing and showed his mother how to hold it against the wound. 'I said you'd stitch it in a couple of hours,' he told Rosalind on his return. 'She's very grateful to you.'

'Hope she stays that way,' Rosalind muttered.

Although she knew she was competent, this gash was going to be difficult. The skin was stretched tightly across the skull and had retracted. There wasn't much flesh to hold the gut underneath. After giving the boy a sedative and spraying with a local anaesthetic, she got to work.

The heat and the presence of the people outside were forgotten. All she had to do was suture. When she'd finished she felt pleased with her work.

'Perfect,' Noah said with satisfaction. He spread two enormous hands and looked at them. 'I couldn't do work so fine. You need little fingers like yours for precision work.'

'Possibly,' she said. 'That was an interesting interlude. Do we have any more work here?'

But Noah thought they'd done enough for the day. Promising to return in the morning, he led Rosalind back across the island. As she walked she now kept a wary eye overhead for possible falling coconuts. She realised she was sticky, dirty, exhausted and exhilarated.

There was a white-clad figure sitting on the verandah when they got back. It was Mark, clad in drill shorts and a white shirt. When he saw them he put his hands on the arms of his chair and attempted to struggle to his feet.

'You stay sitting down,' Rosalind snapped. 'I'm not sure you should be out of bed yet.'

'God protect me from over-officious doctors,' he muttered. 'Just a brief period of convalescence, miss. If I'd stayed in that bed much longer I would have gone mad.' He waved at two other seats which had been brought out. 'Why don't you both sit down and Matilda will bring some fruit juice? How did the day go, Noah?'

'Went well. There are three problems I've referred to you next week, and I watched the neatest bit of suturing I've seen outside an operating theatre.'

Those amazing blue eyes turned on her. 'Getting plenty of practice, soon-to-be Doctor?'

She felt her cheeks warm. 'It seemed... I mean...' Then she realised he was teasing her and felt warmer than ever. But if he was going to tease her she would fight back!

'You look better,' she announced. 'I've never seen you with your clothes on before.'

'Nasty sight, the naked doctor,' he murmured, and they both laughed.

Then she looked more closely. 'And you've trimmed your beard and hair. You appear almost respectable.'

'Not all white men go to pieces in the tropics,' he pointed out. 'I only clean my teeth with whisky every second day.'

He still looked ill. The pain lines around his eyes and mouth were deeper and his cheek bones seemed too close to the skin, but he was certainly better than when she'd first seen him. For a moment she saw him as a man, not a patient. There were an awful lot of things she wanted to know about him.

Matilda came out and handed fruit juice round, then whispered to him. He smiled at her and said, 'In about half an hour, Matilda.' Then he explained. 'Matilda has cooked us all a special dinner—she says it's to celebrate my getting better. I thought you both might like to shower before we dine.'

Rosalind tasted her freshly pressed pineapple juice and realised that she was ravenous.

She hadn't brought many clothes in her little bag. There was a long cape for the wet weather and T-shirts, pareus, shorts and underwear. But for some reason she'd brought one dress, a simple white cotton shift, shot through with a silver thread. It didn't weigh much and it rolled up easily. She decided to wear it tonight.

After showering and shampooing she sat in front of the little mirror fixed to her bedroom wall and put on a touch of make-up, mascara and a pink lipstick. There wasn't much she could do with her red hair but brush it—she'd had it cut efficiently short before she'd come out here. Then, rather shyly, she walked over to where the two men were sitting at a table, brought out and laid by Matilda.

Both rose as she approached. 'You've dressed for dinner,' Mark said, eyeing her dress with obvious approval. 'How smart you look.' It was said in his usual half-mocking way but she felt there was an edge of sincerity underneath.

She shrugged. Probably she was the only white woman he'd seen in the past three months. Obviously he'd be a little taken with her.

He saw her to her seat, then leaned forward and lit two candles. A candle-lit tropical meal! How... romantic?

It was a meal to remember. She already knew that the fruit and vegetables would be of the freshest and the fish would have been caught in the lagoon that afternoon, but there was also pork in the most delicate of fruit sauces. She guessed the food had been cooked in a hot pit in the traditional manner somewhere behind the house. Stones were heated by burning coconut husks and then the food wrapped in banana leaves and placed on top. This gave a taste she'd never experienced before.

From somewhere Mark had found a bottle of white wine, a semi-sparkling Saumur. She knew that this evening would echo in her memory—both for the food and the company.

They had coffee after dinner, then Noah excused himself and set off for the village. He wanted to visit friends, and there were always cases he needed to catch up on.

Rosalind was left alone with Mark, with the distant

pounding of surf on the reef the only sound. For a while they sat in silence, then he said abruptly, 'There's something you can help me with tomorrow if you'd like to.'

She looked at him thoughtfully. 'You've not recovered yet and I don't think you should be working.'

He held his hands in front of his face. 'Not exactly shaking,' he said, 'but I know I'm not at my best and I wouldn't want to harm anybody. Thirty people will call in tomorrow, Rosalind, all expecting to answer a few questions and give some blood. I'll ask the questions but I'd like you to take the samples.'

'Of course I'll do it if Noah doesn't want me.' She considered for a minute. 'Are you going to analyse the blood at once?'

He shrugged. 'Normally I would, but it should keep in the fridge.'

She shook her head. 'No, it should be done at once. I've done a bit of analysis, and I'd like to help with this if you don't mind.'

'I'd be delighted. But you know what this kind of work is like. It's tedious, finicky and time-consuming. Wouldn't you rather see something of the island?'

'I'm here to work and learn,' she said, 'and that's what I'll do.'

He smiled. 'You're a determined young lady. I'll be glad of your help.'

They sat together for a while longer in companionable silence. Then she said, 'Exactly what are you researching? I saw some results on your desk—what have you discovered so far?'

'I'll fetch my raw data.' Before she could stop him he had risen and gone to fetch the ledger she'd glanced at. He looked weary when he returned with the heavy book.

'I could have done that,' she scolded. 'You know, you must stop pushing yourself. You have to take things easy for a while.'

'I like pushing myself. All doctors have to. But I'm a lot better than I used to be, Rosalind.'

'Hmm,' she snorted.

She looked at the rows of neat figures that he showed her. 'The people of this island tend to intermarry. Surprisingly, there have been no problems—no examples of recessive genes producing the conditions we sometimes find in England.'

'Interesting,' she commented as he finally closed the book, 'but there will have to be follow-up studies in a few years. Are you thinking of doing that?'

He glanced out into the deep blue darkness, and leaned back so his face was in shadow. 'No. My time here will be over and I'll go back to England. Perhaps work in Europe or America a while. Research is all very well but really I'm a doctor. I ought to get involved with patients.'

It was said in his customary half-joking tone but she felt— as she felt so often with him—that there might be a current of seriousness underneath.

'What sort of doctor were you? A GP?

'No. I am an FRCS and a senior registrar in general surgery.'

She looked at him in astonishment. 'You shouldn't be here! This research is all very well, but any post-graduate student could do it. Dr Parang would love to have you on the main island—you ought to be helping him there.'

His tone was jesting. 'The thing is, Rosalind, I've been engrossed in medicine since I was fourteen. School, university, teaching hospital—all I've done has been aimed at one end. It's good—sometimes it's necessary—to have a rest.'

'Of course,' she said, though she wasn't convinced. He'd told her part of a story, but she was sure there was something he had missed out.

Perhaps he sensed her doubt. Painfully he got to his feet. 'I think I'll go to bed if you don't mind. You were right, I shouldn't try to overdo things. Matilda will clear up so you sit here and enjoy the evening.'

She stood, too. 'I'm sorry if I overtired you.' She added honestly, 'But I enjoy talking to you.'

It was easier to see his face now, the flickering candles emphasising rather than hiding his expression. And she was sure her words had had an effect on him that was stronger than she had intended. 'And I enjoy talking to you,' he said abruptly. 'It's interesting to meet fellow medical people. Goodnight.' He moved into the house.

For a while she sat on the verandah, thinking about the enigmatic Dr Harrison. Then she told herself she was being foolish. His reasons for coming here were obvious and believable. Why should she think there was anything else?

The next day was fun. With a broad grin Noah told her to enjoy herself—she could come out with him the following day. Dr Mark might need help.

Although still not fully well, Mark seemed to be getting better, but Rosalind made him do as little as possible. With Matilda's help, she laid out the instruments she would need and said all he had to do was sit and write up the answers to the questions.

The first subject was Simoa, a smiling man of about

nineteen stone, with an undeniable sense of his own importance. He was white haired and stripped to the waist,
with his pareu somehow clinging to the underside of a
vast rounded abdomen.

'Simoa is the village headman,' Mark explained.
'Matilda is his daughter. I've picked up a bit of the local
tongue but Simoa speaks English so he's offered to act
as interpreter.'

'Speak English good,' Simoa informed her.

First Mark asked a series of questions about Simoa's
diet. She listened, amazed, to what Simoa thought a necessary amount to be consumed each day. No wonder he
was so heavy! Then she carefully took the blood sample.
She had no difficulty in finding a vein as there were
powerful muscles under the layers of fat.

The rest of the people who were to give blood and
answer questions came drifting in during the morning.
She had noticed the casual attitude to time which most
of the natives had. On the islands it was known as 'coconut time'. But they had always been on time for Noah.
When there was no one present, and Simoa was being
fed a mid-morning snack by his daughter, she asked
Mark about this.

He shrugged. 'They know Noah is only here once
every six months. I'm here all the time. Why hurry today
when you can wander in tomorrow?'

'Doesn't that annoy you? Other people wasting their
time would annoy most doctors I know.'

He nodded thoughtfully. 'It used to make me blaz-
ingly angry. I thought time wasted was time spoiled. But,
really, that's why I came here. I wanted to mix with
people who weren't always in a hurry. Being here has
improved me.'

'You'll always be in a hurry,' she said. 'You won't even obey doctor's orders when you're told to relax or convalesce.'

He grinned. 'You're not a proper doctor yet so I asked for a second opinion. Mine. And I thought I was fit to work.'

She sniffed. 'A doctor who treats himself has a fool for a patient.'

'Ow,' he said, 'that's not fair. Isn't it against the Hippocratic oath to call your patient a fool?'

'Not my patient,' she said sweetly. 'Yours.'

'You're too sharp, young Grey. One day you'll cut yourself with a scalpel.'

Rosalind liked talking to Mark, much more than she did to most men. Nothing appeared to be serious to him, though she suspected that this was a front.

After a moment he asked her, 'Have you noticed how happy the people are here? They're always smiling, laughing, always pleased to see you.'

'Yes, I've noticed,' she said. 'I like it.'

'I think they're happy because nothing ever bothers them. There's always going to be enough fish in the lagoon, enough fruit to pick. So why bother rushing?'

'Because Western civilisation is on its way here,' she said sadly. 'This life won't—can't—last.'

'She's sharp *and* a pessimist,' he said. 'What a doleful combination.'

There was an outburst of giggling from the verandah but no one entered. 'I think we've got another client,' he said, 'but don't rush to pick up your syringe. There's important gossip to be passed on. Matilda hasn't seen her friend since yesterday.'

She said, 'You're a cynic, Dr Harrison.' He winked at her.

She spent the next morning with Noah at the local village, and then the pair of them walked through the groves to the distant settlement to check on the young boy whose scalp she had sutured. Noah peeled away the dressing and they looked at her work. 'That's good,' Noah said. 'Healing nicely. You did a good job there, Miss Rosalind.'

She looked again at the neat stitches crossing the shaven skull, and a small feeling of pride welled up in her. 'It isn't too bad, is it?' she said.

Of course, she'd told Mark about the head wound and how she'd treated it, and when she got back early to his bungalow she was looking forward to telling him how well it looked. Noah had stopped off in the village.

Mark was sitting on the verandah in shirt and shorts again. She waved and he waved back. Before she could detect any expression on his face she knew that something was disturbing him. The tense way he held his body and the stiff way he lifted his arm suggested a man who was not at ease. However, he managed a strained smile as she walked up the steps.

'Had a good day?' he asked.

She flopped into the cane chair opposite him. 'Something's worrying you—what is it?' she demanded.

The smile changed into something with more affection. 'I like you, Dr Rosalind,' he said. 'Always time for niceties, time for the oblique approach to diagnosis. But you're right and I'll tell you what's wrong. I'm bored with sitting here. I want exercise.'

'Exercise is the last thing you want,' she said. 'In your

condition I can think of few worse things. You'd put back your recovery by weeks.'

'I know, I know. Just because something is right doesn't make it pleasant. It's just that I miss my swim in the lagoon.'

She reached over to pat his arm. 'I feel for you, I really do. It must be rotten, missing something like that. Since I got here people have been telling me that I must borrow a pair of fins and a mask and go for a dive. I've just not—'

'You haven't been diving in the lagoon yet?' His expression was almost comic in its disbelief.

'Well, there's so much else to do and see and I—'

'Go and change into your bathing costume and— You have brought something to swim in?' This time his expression suggested that there were some things that weren't even conceivable.

'Of course,' she said huffily, 'but I'm certain you shouldn't—'

It wasn't her day for finishing sentences. 'We're going on a guided tour,' he said, and turned to shout, 'Matilda, go fetch Bika!'

This wasn't the tough metal dinghy with an outboard that she'd travelled in with Noah. This was a real native wooden canoe with an outrigger, held together, apparently, with wire and what looked suspiciously like string.

Mark sat in the bow facing her. A cheerful man called Bika sat in the stern and paddled the canoe to the centre of the lagoon with strong, experienced arms.

The sun was hot overhead. Behind her was the green fringe of the island and in front of her the hiss of waves breaking on the reef. The lagoon was mirror-calm. She stared at Mark's calm figure.

'You're not to swim,' she stated.

Now that he was doing something, even if it was only being taken for a ride in a canoe, he seemed more at ease with himself. 'I have no intention of swimming,' he said silkily. 'My doctor wouldn't approve. But you can swim. You can use fins and a mask, I take it?'

The borrowed equipment fitted her perfectly. 'I've had some practice,' she said.

'Good. Now, remember, you're not on your own. Bika and I will watch everything you do and Bika could swim for twelve hours, carrying you on his back. Roll over the side, swim down a few feet and look around.'

She sat there a moment, then she threw off the towel she'd been clutching round her shoulders and splashed into the water.

Of course, she'd known what to expect. She'd seen colour prints without number of the vivid coral, the fish, the waving seaweed, but it was all immeasurably better in reality.

The water caressed her and supported her as she twisted and rolled past a great tree of pink coral. A shoal of tiny silver fish faced her, then turned and fled as one. Reluctantly she returned to the surface.

'It's wonderful,' she called, hanging onto the outrigger. 'I'm going back down again.'

'Just take an ordinary breath, don't hyperventilate,' he said. 'That way you won't tire.'

She dived, and this time swam straight through the cloud of tiny fish. It seemed impossible that so many of them could avoid her—but they all did.

To show she'd dived so far she picked up a shell from the seabed and kicked back to the surface. Mark frowned. 'I wouldn't pick anything up until you're quite sure about it,' he said. 'Heard of the stonefish?'

Even in the warm water she shuddered. The poison of the stonefish caused almost unendurable agony. 'I'll be careful,' she said.

For half an hour she dived and explored, always aware of the hull of the canoe above her and the two pair of eyes watching her. She felt free but secure. Underwater was a wonderland and, like Peter Pan, she could fly through it.

Finally Mark said, 'One more dive and then that's it. You'll be surprised at how tired you are later.'

'But I feel great!'

'One more dive. Believe me, I'm right.'

So she allowed herself to be hauled aboard, and Mark wrapped the towel around her as Bika paddled to the shore.

She was still exhilarated as she walked up the beach with Mark and entered the coolness of the shady mangroves. 'I wouldn't have done that if it hadn't been for you,' she said, 'and it was wonderful. Thank you!'

On impulse she wrapped her arms around him and kissed him.

She'd meant it as a friendly gesture, to kiss him as she might have kissed one of her brothers-in-law. She tried to squeeze his broad chest, not bothering that her wet costume would dampen his shirt.

The kiss lasted. One hand slid under her towel to hold her naked back while the other cupped her neck. She pressed closer to him, her eyes closed. Her lips parted under the sweet pressure of his. She didn't want to move or think. She wanted to stay here, being kissed.

Gently he pushed her away from him. For a moment

they stared at each other, and in his eyes she saw a flash of vulnerability she'd never seen before. Then it was gone.

'I must take you diving again,' he said, in his old familiar sardonic tone, 'if you're going to kiss me every time.'

Half-sadly, she recognised that treating it casually was the best way to deal with what had just happened between them. 'Just the one kiss,' she said. 'I don't really approve of men with beards.'

'Not suitable for a doctor,' he agreed. 'Now, I'll bet you're ravenous.'

She was. As he led her back through the grove she tried to concentrate on the meal to come. It stopped her thinking of the effect of Mark's kiss.

She slept well that night. Mark went to bed early, saying that he felt tired, and she went shortly afterwards. The next day she went out with Noah as they were busy, trying to fit in all that he'd not yet done.

'We could manage all in two days,' Noah said, 'if people would come to the clinic at once. They're better than they used to be but...' He shrugged.

She watched the last laughing family walk away. 'It's a different kind of life,' she said. 'I'll bet you don't get many stress-related illnesses here.'

He grinned. 'Never seen one case yet.'

When they returned they had their evening meal with Mark, who then looked over the list of cases Noah wanted him to check on in the next couple of weeks.

'If you don't mind,' Noah said.

Mark shook his head. 'Whatever I can do to help.' Again he went to bed early, saying he was sure his doctor would approve.

Noah walked down to the village and Rosalind was left feeling rather down. She thought Mark was deliberately avoiding her. Perhaps she shouldn't have kissed him.

The next day was their last on Malapa. Mark walked down to the beach with them, and as Noah and a crowd of villagers carried the boat into the water Rosalind had a last quick word with him.

'You know, you're still not well,' she said professionally, 'but you should be all right if you take things easy.'

'I know that. I've been treated and counselled by a good doctor.'

'Don't say that! I'm not one yet.'

Seriously, he said, 'You will be a doctor and I think you'll be a good one. Certainly you'll be an excellent clinician—but that's not the same as being a good doctor. You've got a keen, analytic mind, but being a doctor means feeling as well as thinking.'

'Medicine is a science before it's an art,' she said.

'I think I'd have to disagree, but there we go. Have a good trip. Medicine is a small world and perhaps we'll bump into each other when I get back to England.'

She felt a quickly stifled touch of sadness. She'd wondered if he would offer to write to her or even ask her to write to him.

The dinghy was now afloat and Noah had started the engine.

'Time to go,' she said. She looked at him, still with the lines of illness on his face, but otherwise looking well. Inconsequentially, she decided that his blue eyes *were* the same colour as the sea. An undefined emotion swept through her—she didn't quite know what she was feeling. She decided it was the result of fatigue and the strangeness of her surroundings.

'I don't want to kiss a man with a beard,' she said firmly. She'd decided to forget the incident in the grove as he so obviously wanted to do just that. 'But my family hug a lot. D'you mind if I hug you?'

Mark opened his arms and for a brief moment she clung to the muscular chest and the trim waist. He was hard in her embrace, and she could smell soap and, because it was a hot day, the scent of man underneath. It had only been meant to be a brief hug, but she found it comforting and perhaps stayed there longer than she should.

She broke away. 'Thanks for what you did for me,' she said hurriedly, and turned to splash out to the canoe. Willing hands helped her aboard, the motor rattled and the screw bit into the water. She was leaving.

He remained on the beach as they moved out towards the gap in the reef. After a while he waved one last time and she waved back. He didn't move until he was just a dot on the silver-sanded beach.

Rosalind wasn't sure what she was feeling. Mark was older than her—ten years older, he'd told her. She'd probably never see him again, but she'd found him disturbing, unsettling. She would put him firmly out of her mind—she'd never had difficulty doing this. Mark Harrison, his illness and the island had been an episode in her past which was now over.

That night, when she was once more safely aboard the government steamer, she wrote up her journal. Her observations were strictly formal. Her elective would be soon over, then she had eighteen months' hard work before she became a real doctor.

CHAPTER THREE

THE little crowd of young people in the corridor was obviously uneasy.

There were a few murmured conversations but most people tended to remain silent. One man, with a white face and glassy eyes which suggested a previous evening's solid drinking, swaggered towards them, shouting, 'Is this where the hanging is?' No one laughed or even looked at him. He, too, lapsed into silence and glumly leaned against the wall.

A door opened and the crowd moved back to let a woman out of an office. She gave a quick sympathetic smile to those who were looking desperately at her—and at the sheet of paper in her hand. Her shoes clicked on the tiles as she walked to the noticeboard and pinned up a single sheet of paper. Then she wriggled through those pressing round her. The first voice was heard—jubilant, ecstatic. 'I've passed!'

Rosalind waited until the crowd had thinned, before making her way to see her name on the pass list. She gave a cool nod and a smile. She'd passed all right.

'Congratulations, Ros, we both made it!' Rosalind's friend, Alison Barnes, picked her up and kissed her. Alison's height of six feet made her ebullience even more attractive. She'd kissed everybody else in the crowd—in fact, there was an awful lot of kissing going on.

'We're all going to the Britannia to celebrate a bit

later,' Alison went on. 'Just for once you can break your rule about midday drinking and come with us.'

'I certainly will,' Rosalind said. She looked round at the rapidly disappearing group. For five years she'd been with them, getting on with some and disliking others. She'd shared in their hopes and their disappointments. Now they were to part. It wasn't an ending, she told herself, but something new beginning.

Most people were going to phone friends, family or lovers with their good news. She supposed she ought to let her sisters know but tonight would do.

'I'm just going to phone Harold,' Alison said. 'He won't like being dragged out of class but it's not every day his fiancée becomes a doctor. Wait for me, kid, won't be a second.'

Rosalind had met Harold, Alison's long-time fiancé, at a hospital dance. He was a senior classics teacher in an expensive local private school. He was very clever but privately Rosalind thought he was a bit of a snob.

'Is he happy for you?' she asked when Alison returned after what had seemed to be a very brief telephone conversation.

Alison looked thoughtfully at her engagement ring. 'He'd better be,' she said shortly. She made an obvious effort to change her mood. 'Come on, let's see if someone falls over in the street then we can push our way to the front of the crowd, shouting, "Let me through, I'm a doctor."'

'I can hardly wait,' Rosalind said drily. 'I like my patients in a clinic or a ward. I don't want to practise medicine on a pavement.'

'Fair comment.' Alison looked curiously at her friend. 'You know, we're all happy—relieved that we've passed. But you're not surprised at the result, are you? You knew you would get through.'

Rosalind shrugged. 'I'd prepared for all the questions that came up. I thought I'd answered them quite well.'

'I know you worked—Lord, how you did work. But I still wish I had some of your confidence.'

'The prof said that overconfidence was the ruin of more doctors than drink was,' Rosalind reminded her with a smile.

But Alison's attention was elsewhere. 'Look at poor Eddie Marsh.' At the far end of the corridor was the solitary figure of the man whose brash remarks had irritated the others. If anything, his face was whiter than before. His name had not been on the list. He was the only candidate to fail. 'He's not coming to the Britannia with us.'

'It must be the first drink he's turned down in his life,' Rosalind said harshly.

Alison turned in shock. 'Don't you feel just a bit sorry for him?' she asked.

In fact, there were good reasons why Rosalind wasn't sorry for him. Eddie had sneered that she was certain to pass—with two specialist registrars in her family, someone was bound to tell her the questions that would come up. However, that wasn't Alison's concern.

'He can retake the exam,' she told Alison. 'If he'd spent less time drinking and playing football he could have passed this time.'

Alison blinked. 'Bit uncharitable, isn't it?' she asked.

Silently Rosalind tried to remind herself that saying what she felt wasn't always the most tactful thing to do. 'Just let me ask one question,' she said. 'If you were brought into an accident and emergency department with internal injuries, and you found Eddie leaning over you, how would you feel?'

Alison didn't need to think long. 'Point taken,' she said. 'I guess he didn't deserve to pass. Come on. Let's go and celebrate.'

They walked through the corridor of the medical school into the hall of the teaching hospital. Rosalind looked up at the modern galleried great hall, felt the people eddying around her. There were nurses, doctors, clerks, porters, patients, policemen, cleaners, ambulance-men, all with their part to play in life of the hospital.

She wasn't a learner any more. Now she was a player. Rosalind always tried to be cool, not let her emotions show. Emotions were messy things. But suddenly she felt a great feeling of excitement. She slid her arm around Alison's waist and squeezed her. 'I'm a doctor!' she cried.

Faces turned to look at her, some surprised and some, knowing that the results had just come out, smiling.

'There you are,' said Alison. 'I knew you were human after all.'

It was a good party. Rosalind didn't dance very often, but when she did she loved it. To celebrate she'd bought a new dress in a rich burgundy silk, which swirled around her knees as she managed another swift pirouette.

Usually she wouldn't spend this much on a dress but, then, it wasn't every month that she became a doctor, and it really set off her flame-red hair. She'd had her hair dressed, too, she liked it.

She caught a glimpse of herself in the mirror in the hall and was surprised how she looked. Her hair, loose for once, waved and billowed. The Indian choker, borrowed from her sister and called liquid silver echoed the colour of her eyes. She looked, well, almost abandoned. And that wasn't her—she was always in control.

She never drank to excess, but tonight she had had just a touch more than she normally would have taken. Her brother-in-law, Alex, had given her champagne, and she loved it. It sparkled and it made her sparkle, too.

The party was in the house of her sister, Lisa. They had a large, old-fashioned house with a big living room, opening into an equally big dining room. Together the two rooms provided a fair-sized dance floor. At one end Lisa's step-daughter, Holly, ran a disco with determined efficiency.

Rosalind had two sisters. Lisa, the older, had been a sister at Blazes, the local hospital, and had married Alex Scott, the specialist registrar in infectious diseases there. Alex had two children already, Holly and Jack. Now the entire family was looking forward to Lisa's first baby, due in three months.

The next sister, Emily, was a midwife, and she'd married Stephen James, a gynaecologist.

The three sisters had always been very close. Rosalind had wondered if things would change when her sisters got married, but they hadn't. They were the same—but different.

Rosalind was dancing with Will Roberts, a doctor two years older than her, a senior house officer in the university hospital. He was, she supposed, her boyfriend. She'd been with him longer than any other boyfriend— not that she'd had so many.

She whirled around again in another pirouette, and glanced at his reflection in the mirror. Will was tall, slim—thin, even. His hair was arranged carefully and his handsome face was solemn. Will did everything carefully—that was why he was such a good doctor. In a room full of casual dressers he was wearing a suit.

'Enjoying yourself?' Rosalind asked, wrapping her arms around his waist.

He appeared to consider the question. Then, eventually, he said with a small smile, 'of course.'

Rosalind tried to tempt him into even wilder dancing, Will wouldn't have it. 'There are senior medical people here,' he muttered to her. 'They might notice.' Will didn't want to look a fool—it might harm his career.

The Beatles' 'Twist and Shout' came to an end, and with solemn expertise Holly started 'I will always love you,' by Dionne Warwick. At the same time the lights dimmed.

'I've got a lighting plan to match the mood of the music,' she'd told Rosalind. 'Is there anything you specially want me to play?'

Will's arm slid further round her as they gently swayed to the music. 'Good of your sisters to arrange this for you,' he said.

'I know,' Rosalind said.

'Looking forward to being a houseman?'

Why did Will manage to ask the same questions as everybody else?

'Very much so.'

'You'll be frantically busy.'

Everybody had told her that too. She didn't feel like commenting again.

'It might be a good time to make an announcement,' Will said. 'This is a turning point, you becoming a doctor. Your life is changing, perhaps in more ways than one.'

She knew what he meant. As ever, Will was approaching things cautiously. 'You mean we should say we're getting engaged?' she asked boldly.

He didn't like her being so brutally frank. 'Well, something like that,' he said. 'You know it's time I was thinking of settling down, and you ought to as well. And now you have to concentrate on your work...'

'You know, Will, you're a real romantic,' she said drily. 'That was a proposal I shall treasure.'

He flinched at her irony. 'I thought that's one thing we had in common,' he protested. 'We're neither of us easily moved by emotion, we're clear, rational human beings.'

She knew that was how a lot of people saw her, and usually the idea pleased her, but she wasn't so sure tonight.

Pulling her closer, Will said, 'Well, we have an understanding, don't we?'

Perhaps they did—she wasn't sure. She quite liked him, if only because he always treated her as an equal, but...she pulled away as the track ended. 'Would you like to meet Alex, my brother-in-law?' she asked. 'He's the one who's a specialist registrar in infectious diseases.'

'I certainly would,' Will said, and his face lit up. Like her, he usually didn't like parties. He hadn't been keen on this one until he'd found out how many senior medical staff would be present.

After making the introduction, Rosalind excused herself and slipped away to the kitchen. There she found her pregnant sister, Lisa, and her other sister, Emily, happily surveying the mountain of food they'd prepared.

'I'll help,' Rosalind said. 'You can't cope with this by yourselves.'

Lisa made shooing noises. 'Go away, party girl. It's your turn to enjoy yourself. You can help wash up later.'

Rosalind grabbed a pinny anyway. 'Will's talking to Alex about medical things. He'll be quite happy without me for a while.'

'You've seen quite a bit of Will recently,' Emily put in. 'Is he going to be the man? We've almost given up hope of pairing you off, and we fancy another wedding.'

Is he the man? Rosalind asked herself. She didn't know. 'I suppose he could be,' she hedged. 'He has a lot of good points.'

'If you're that detached about it, he isn't,' Lisa said forcefully. 'If you're in love you'll know it.'

'I'm always detached,' Rosalind answered calmly, and decided to ignore the way her sisters grinned knowingly at each other. 'Anyway, Emily, where's Stephen? I haven't seen him yet.'

'Usual problem—work,' Emily said, resigned but happy. 'He phoned to say he'd be late. Now, take off that pinny and go out and socialise! We're putting the food out now.'

Several couples were dancing but there were plenty of people to chat to. She stopped to talk to Sir Arthur Miles, the infectious diseases consultant at Blazes, an old friend of her sister and her husband.

'It's a pity your father couldn't be here,' Sir Arthur said. 'What's the latest news about him?'

Some time ago Rosalind's father had been kidnapped by guerillas in South America, but he'd become friendly with his captors, and had decided to stay with them voluntarily when the government had offered them peace.

'He's coming home soon.' Rosalind's face lit up. 'He says he's written a book about his experiences. It'll be lovely to see him.'

'I look forward to meeting him,' Sir Arthur said. 'Any man who could father and bring up three daughters the way he has— well, he must be quite a person.'

'He's lovely,' Rosalind said.

Sir Arthur looked around. 'Not a lot of your fellows here,' he commented. 'Where are all the others who have just graduated?'

She grinned. 'Over the hills and far away. For a lot of them it's the first chance of a big holiday in years.'

'And you decided not to go on holiday?'

She shrugged. 'I'm looking forward to starting work. I've done some reading, managed to look in on one or two wards. I'm going to do my housemanship in Blazes, you know.'

'I know. Surgical ward for the first six months. If you do your second six months in a medical ward, let me know. I'll offer you a place.'

She shook her head. 'Too close to family. I don't want to work with my brother-in-law.'

'You should, you'd learn a lot from him.'

He leaned over to pat her arm. 'Medicine is a twenty-four-hour lifetime sentence,' he said gently. 'You should rest while you can.'

'I don't like resting.'

There was the bustle of someone arriving in the hall so she excused herself and went to greet her new guests. She was just in time to see Emily kiss her newly arrived husband and greet another man.

'Why have you been missing my party?' she asked her brother-in-law. 'You've got to dance with me.'

Stephen turned and hugged her. 'Hello, little sister Doctor. I've missed your party to be with another female. Baby Thomasina decided to gatecrash this world three months early and I stayed on to help her.'

'Three months?' Rosalind asked thoughtfully. 'A thirty week pre-term. That's about the limit, isn't it?'

'Fairly close, though viability can be sustained earlier. We had to intubate her, and when the apex beat fell below sixty I gave her external cardiac massage. But now baby Thomasina's alive, kicking and putting up a good fight.' He winked. 'When you're thinking of specialising gynaecology has its moments.'

She turned as someone else entered the hall. Her sister's voice said, 'Get Stephen to take you in and introduce you to a few people.'

It was the newcomer, the man who had entered with Stephen. She couldn't make him out clearly as the hall was dimly lit and the bright light of the kitchen behind turned him into a silhouette.

He was a tall man, strongly built. As he came closer she saw he was dressed casually but well in black trousers and a mid-blue shirt. From the way the shirt hung, she guessed it was linen. His short hair was a dark blond colour.

She was sure she knew him but she didn't know from where. This irritated her—she should have remembered such an interesting man. Then he spoke. The moment she heard that sardonic, teasing tone, a voice that suggested nothing should be taken seriously, she recognised him at once.

What a contrast from the raffish man she had met on the island of Malapa, all those thousands of miles away! He came further into the light, and she saw that his face was now less drawn, but, of course, he still had those startling bright blue eyes. What was Mark Harrison doing here?

'I remember what you said when we parted,' he said. 'You said your family hug a lot. And I gather there's cause for celebration so may I give you a congratulatory hug?'

'Yes,' she whispered.

It was different from being hugged by her brother-in-law. Both were big men, both were strong, and neither would try to impress by sheer strength. But when Mark pulled her gently towards him and she felt his firm hand on her waist and leaned against the muscular arch of his chest it just wasn't the same. Hugging Stephen didn't produce this riot of unexplained feelings in her. For a second she felt her normal coolness desert her.

She was enjoying being held against him but it was having an effect on her so she carefully moved away. She was the calm, poised Rosalind Grey. Nothing ever flurried her—certainly not being hugged by a man!

'I'll go and get you a drink, Mark,' Stephen said with a grin. 'You old friends must have a lot of catching up to do.'

Mark hadn't yet let go of her hands. They looked at each other for a moment then she freed herself completely. It was just such a shock.

'What are you doing here?' she asked. It was a banal question, but the only one she could think of.

His voice was the same as ever. 'What am I doing here? I like parties. And your sister's food is famous throughout the hospital. And your brother-in-law is my friend. But, young Doctor Grey, the old doctor never sleeps. This is business. I came to check up on my firm's latest recruit.'

She couldn't help herself. She squeaked, '*Your* firm?'

'Certainly. I'm Specialist Registrar on the surgical firm you've joined. You'll be seeing a lot of me.'

She didn't know how she felt but she forced herself to be calm and said, 'Well, that'll be…fun.'

Was 'fun' the word she wanted?

He went on remorselessly, 'And I know you'll behave and work hard. If you don't I'll report you to the GMC for practising medicine before you're qualified.'

'Practising medicine!'

'You may have saved my life, young Grey, prescribing antibiotics and cutting into my shoulder, but you didn't have that certificate that now hangs above the bedstead.'

'I'm beginning to think that saving your life wasn't such a good idea!'

'You will find that problem in a lot of medicine. I've brought round more than a few drunken drivers who…'

Stephen appeared, gave Mark a glass of champagne and raised his eyebrows questioningly at Rosalind. She shook her head. 'Not for me, thanks. My system has had enough shocks for a while.'

'Then I'll leave you two to get reacquainted. I need food!'

After a pause she said, 'Did I save your life?'

'Possibly. Noah would have done what he could, perhaps even radioed for help, but he wouldn't have know the right dose of antibiotics. I was grateful you were there. Anyway, you're a real doctor now. You'll save lots and lots of lives.'

Suddenly she grinned and poked him with her finger.

'You know, I didn't practise medicine on my own. I had a licensed and qualified doctor with me, presumably supervising. The fact that he went to sleep was his fault, not mine.'

He looked mournful. 'You're too clever for me, Doctor. I can see we're going to have difficulty deciding who is in charge of this firm. We don't want insubordination from the lower ranks. Would you like to dance?'

His invitation came as a surprise to her. She had been enjoying their conversation. He took her arm and led her into the dance area. Just as they arrived a wild and noisy number ended and Holly continued with her policy of alternating the loud and fast with the slow and smoochy. This time it was a very old favourite, Frank Sinatra singing 'One more for the Road'.

Mark looked at Holly disapprovingly. 'I don't know if I can dance to this,' he said.

'You can,' Rosalind instructed. 'Put your arms around my waist and do what the music tells you.'

'It's telling me to go to sleep.' At that moment Holly dimmed the lights. Indignantly he said, 'See, there's a conspiracy to make me sleep. Just when I was going to enjoy myself.'

'How were you going to enjoy yourself?'

'I was going to engage you in a native war dance I learned on the island. That music was just right—same tempo, same simplicity of diction. The natives used to sing a song just like that before they went head-hunting.'

'You're kidding me.'

'Would I, Dr Grey? The natives were head-hunters within living memory.'

As ever, when talking to him, she had difficulty in

deciding when he was being serious and when he wasn't. She rather liked the uncertainty. 'Just dance,' she said. 'Everyone else is.'

In fact, she soon realised that he had been joking about his dancing skills. Although she enjoyed dancing, she didn't have much chance herself, and she wasn't always lucky in her partners. She would have been perfectly happy to nestle against Mark's shoulder but he wasn't content merely to shift weight from one foot to another. He had a real sense of rhythm. They moved slowly but they were dancing, with bodies as well as feet. She liked it.

She caught herself, told herself to stop dreaming—there was lot she needed to know. 'How come you're here?' she asked. 'Why this hospital?'

He looked confused. 'I thought you knew. Dr Parang wrote to his old teaching hospital, saying that an American foundation had offered him funds for a research project and was anyone interested? I was working at the university then so I jumped at the chance. Then I came back here and transferred to Blazes.'

She realised there was a lot she didn't know about him but she thought he might have mentioned that they were so close.

'Have you finished your project?'

He nodded. 'It's written up and submitted.'

'Could I read it?'

He laughed. 'You'll have plenty of other work to occupy you in the next few months. But, yes, I'll lend you a copy.'

'I'll be interested, but I still think the work could have been done by someone less able than you. Your surgical skills were needed on the main island.'

They were close, holding each other. She could feel the warmth of his body against her breasts and her hips and the clasp of his arms around her so she felt the involuntary jerk his body gave. It wasn't much, but it was there. Something she'd said had upset him, but when she looked up his face was as calm as ever.

'You can get stale in medicine,' he said. 'Every now and again it is good to have a change. That's what I did.'

She didn't think too much of his explanation. It might be true but it wasn't the entire story. She wondered if she should ask Stephen about him—the two were obviously friends. Then she decided not to. If Mark wanted to tell her something then he would, but if he didn't she guessed there would be some good reason.

'One more for the road,' sang Frank Sinatra, and the number ended.

Mark didn't let Rosalind go. His grasp was casual and she felt comfortable. If he wanted to dance with her again then she was perfectly happy to oblige.

The lights went up and Holly put on a faster track which started with a deafening drum solo. It was a modern piece that she didn't recognise. They danced again. She found his skills weren't confined to the slow pieces. He moved gracefully, holding and guiding her. It was a long time since she'd enjoyed herself so much on a dance floor.

'You're a good dancer,' she complimented him.

'I told you, I was taught by my head-hunting friends. At the end of this dance I shall cross my eyes and stick out my tongue.'

To her amazement and hilarity he did just that. She laughed aloud.

'This,' he confided as they whirled round a corner, 'paralyses my enemies with fear. They can't escape. Makes hunting heads an awful lot less effort.' They skimmed around the room again. 'Speaking of enemies,' he went on, 'who is the young man who looks as if he wants to hunt *my* head?'

She'd quite forgotten she was supposed to be here with a partner. 'That's Will Roberts,' she said. 'He's a senior house officer—he wants to be an anaesthetist.'

'Ah. So I can have my head hunted painlessly. Has he a proprietorial interest in you?'

She discovered she didn't want to tell Mark that Will was her boyfriend. She temporised. 'He brought me here. We see quite a lot of each other.'

'I see. Then the calmness of old age must give way to the impetuosity of youth. At the end of this you may rejoin him and I will go to eat.'

She squeezed his hand on impulse. 'I'm glad you've come to my party, and you're not old.'

'Ten years older than you, my dear. Introduce me to the young man so he will see he has nothing to fear.'

'I wish you'd be serious sometimes,' she said, though she wasn't sure if she meant it.

Will, of course, was perfectly civil. He'd hidden the look of ill-temper that both she and Mark had noticed and was only too pleased to be introduced to a senior member of the hospital staff. The two men shook hands, exchanged a few courteous words and then Mark wandered off to get something to eat while she danced with Will. Rosalind wasn't sure why she felt irritated.

'I've met Dr Harrison before,' she told Will. 'I like him and I'm looking forward to working with him.'

Will frowned. 'He's a good-looking man. You'd better be careful, he's got the reputation of being a bit of a ladies' man.'

'Are you sure about that?' Rosalind asked. She was surprised at her feelings of disappointment.

Will was sure—he knew all the hospital gossip. 'Absolutely certain,' he said. 'I don't think he'll bother you now, though. After all, he knows you're with me. And he knows your family, too. You'll be all right.'

'I can look after myself,' Rosalind said, irritated yet further. At the far end of the room she could see Mark, plate in hand, chatting to Lisa and Alex. They looked a happy, friendly trio.

She felt disappointed in Mark and angry at herself for being disappointed. What was he to her?

CHAPTER FOUR

IT WASN'T much of a room. There was a bed, wardrobe and chest of drawers, desk and bookshelf. The view was a bit depressing—a bit of car park and the blank end of the laundry. For the next twelve months it would be Rosalind's home so she put up a couple of pictures and arranged her books and her notes. She knew she'd be happy here. She was a doctor, living near her work, so it was better than a palace. She was even getting paid!

The room was in the residency. All housemen were expected to live there as they were often on call. There were supposed to be new rules about the maximum number of hours a houseman could be called on to do, but she knew that if work was there she'd do it.

She had provisionally registered with the General Medical Council, which licensed her as a 'preregistration' doctor. She had joined a medical defence union. So many doctors were being sued now it was necessary to be insured. She had joined the British Medical Association, which, she supposed, was her trade union. There was a lot of paperwork involved to become a doctor.

Officially she'd start on the ward on the next day, but she'd had a little note from Mark in her pigeon hole, saying he'd like to meet her and the other two housemen for a brief preliminary chat. His secretary had phoned to confirm she could come. It was in ten minutes.

She was looking forward to the meeting for reasons

other than medical ones. She wondered about Mark. When she'd seen him at her party he had seemed more relaxed, more outgoing than he'd been on the island. Of course, he *had* been ill when she'd first met him, but she did think there'd been a change in his character.

She had only managed the briefest of further conversations with him at her party. For a start, Will had hardly left her side. But Mark had said how much he was looking forward to working with her, and there had been a gleam in his blue eyes that had suggested he'd meant it.

After Will had said Mark was a womaniser she'd decided she didn't like him. Casual sex was always a temptation in hospitals. People were thrown together, working irregular hours, often in life-or-death situations. Also, some doctors took advantage of their senior positions and the respect in which they were still held.

But was what Will had said true? Mark was certainly attractive, and probably could have his pick of women in the hospital. And his ironic, non-serious attitude to life made it hard to think of him settling down to a permanent relationship.

But… She blushed at the memory. On the island he'd kissed her—or she had kissed him. But in no way had he tried to take advantage of her. If anything, he'd avoided her afterwards. It was odd. She was sure she could feel a basic sensitivity in him.

It felt good to walk into the doctors' commonroom. Now she entered as of right, not by invitation. The other two housemen were there, her friend, Alison Barnes, and a silent, plodding boy called Eric Hart. They greeted each other, helped themselves to coffee and biscuits and found a private corner to sit.

Rosalind hadn't seen Alison for a while, but she knew

she'd been away with her fiancé. She thought Alison looked troubled. She was browner but thinner and seemed on edge. There'd be time to catch up on things later.

Mark came into the commonroom, saw them and waved. He was dressed casually again in jeans and a red checked shirt. Like them, he helped himself to coffee and biscuits.

Rosalind felt a sudden spurt of excitement as he approached. He looked so clean-cut, so amiable. Working with him was going to be fun!

'I just wanted a quick, informal chat,' he said as he sank into a nearby chair. 'I suspect you'll be seeing more of me than Mr Edwards, who is technically the consultant in charge of you. He's got clinics to run, and committees and visits here and there. I'll be more on the spot.'

He sipped his coffee and smiled at them benevolently. 'If there's any problem you'll first ask the senior house officer. He'll usually be handy. But now, for the first time in your lives, you'll be making life-or-death decisions. You can't avoid it, it goes with the job. If you're the slightest bit unsure, bleep the SHO or me. We'll never be angry if you're genuinely in doubt.

'The second thing is, you might think this is a dogsbody's job. You're there for everybody to tread on. This is true. But the job is vital. The houseman is the link between nurses, porters, therapists, GPs, relatives—even important people like me. We all come to you for information about the patient.'

He took a digestive biscuit from his plate, looked at it gloomily and broke it in half. Then he gave half to

Rosalind, took her chocolate biscuit and broke off half for himself.

'Always remember,' he said seriously, 'that the last chocolate biscuit is left for senior staff.'

Eric and Alison looked at him, amazed; Rosalind was less surprised.

He went on. 'Keep all your paperwork up to date. More doctors have made mistakes through inadequate note-taking than through bad diagnosis.

'And, last of all, remember that medicine is an art as well as a science. Science deals with facts, art deals with people. You're dealing with people, not diseases. It isn't a gangrenous foot in bed nine. She's Amy Jones, who has a job, a family and worries. OK, sermon over. Any questions?'

Rosalind thought he'd handled the meeting well, and felt more relaxed and confident about starting. She could tell that Alison and Eric felt the same way. Especially Alison. She looked a lot happier than when she came in.

'What do we call you?' Alison asked.

'In front of patients, I think, Doctor or Mr Harrison. A bit of formality reassures them. But the rest of the time plain Mark.' He pursed his lips thoughtfully. 'I suggest you call the consultant Mr Edwards. He's old—even older than me.'

Eric then asked some ponderous question about hours of work. 'I'll never ask you for more than you can give,' Mark answered him, 'but I don't expect a newly qualified doctor to be a clock-watcher.'

His bleeper sounded. He checked the number on the display then ruefully said, 'This will happen constantly so get used to it. I'm needed on the ward. See you there tomorrow.'

'May I walk over with you?' Eric asked.

The two men disappeared, leaving Alison with Rosalind.

'Isn't he lovely?' Alison asked. 'Those gorgeous blue eyes with that dark blond hair. And he's so tanned!'

Rosalind agreed, but she wasn't going to say so. 'I don't know whether he's handsome or not,' she said noncommittally, 'but I think he'll make a good teacher.'

She chaffed her friend gently. 'But you shouldn't have eyes for other men. What would Harold say? How is he, anyway, and how was your holiday?'

Alison said, 'I've spent most of the last few years snatching hours with him when I could, and at long last we had weeks we could spend together.'

She showed Rosalind her left hand. It was brown— apart from the white band round the finger where a ring used to be. 'We didn't get on and so we've split up.'

'I'm sorry,' said Rosalind gently. I shouldn't have asked. Perhaps it's only temporary? A lovers' disagreement?'

'I doubt it. It seems pretty permanent to me.'

Alison looked decidedly upset. Rosalind wondered why so many women of her acquaintance got into a state about men. It would certainly never happen to her.

Next day was Rosalind's first as a doctor. She was up early and dressed sensibly in a cool dress and flat shoes. Just before she left her room she put on a long white coat which she'd picked up the day before. It gave her a thrill. Students wore short white coats. A long coat was her badge of office.

Mark wasn't waiting for her on Ward 9.

'He was up all night dealing with a ruptured aortic

aneurism,' Sister Talbot said. 'He's gone to get some rest. But here's what he wants you to do.' She presented Rosalind with a list. 'It's bloods first.'

She'd done this before. A sample of blood had to be taken from each patient and sent down to the laboratory for analysis. She went to the first patient, reassured her and asked to see the inside of her arm. This one would be easy as the blue vein was prominent. After swabbing with antiseptic, she eased in the needle and pulled back the plunger. The syringe filled with dark blood. 'That's all.' She smiled at the patient. 'No trouble, was it?'

It usually wasn't a hard job. There was always someone who would call her the lady vampire and there was always one arm where the vein was hard to find, but this time the round was straightforward. She was making good time. She stopped by the sister's desk to find someone to take the samples down to the lab.

'Are you the doctor?' a disbelieving voice behind her said. 'I'd like a word.' Sister Talbot smiled a small mischievous smile and sat behind her desk.

The speaker was a fat, unshaven man aged about forty. His white shirt was rumpled and he held a plastic cup of coffee. He wasn't very happy when he discovered that Rosalind was the only doctor on the ward, but decided that she'd have to do.

'It's my grandad,' the man went on, 'Mr Chester. I'm Mr Chester, too. He was brought in after a fall this morning and when he wakes up he'll just walk out of here. He's never been good at staying in, and keeping him in bed will kill him so I want to know what you're going to do about it.' He looked at her belligerently.

Rosalind reached for the case notes that Sister Talbot

silently held out and followed Mr Chester to his grand-father's bedside.

After a quick glance at the patient and the notes she decided that there wasn't much chance of Mr Chester, the grandfather, walking out of the ward. He was eighty-five and had been brought in by ambulance at three in the morning. A and E had decided he had a fractured hip, and he was down for a pin and plate later in the day.

'Your grandfather has had a very nasty fall,' she said, 'but things seem to be proceeding quite well. We should be able to discharge him in a week or two.'

'He won't stand it. He'll sign himself out.'

'He'll be in some discomfort when he wakes, Mr Chester. I doubt he'll want to leave. I doubt he'll be able to.'

'You don't know him.'

The irritating thing was that she recognised that Mr Chester was motivated by a genuine regard for his grandfather but it took her twenty minutes to persuade him that there was nothing he could do but go home and return later.

'Yes,' she said finally, 'I guarantee that he won't sign himself out. Yes, I will stop him in person. See you later, Mr Chester.'

Is this the kind of medicine I want to practise? she asked herself. Then she remembered Mark's advice—these were people not diseases.

Two more cases were being admitted to the ward for operations the next day, and after the nurse had showed them their beds Rosalind had to clerk them. Fortunately they were well documented already so she only had to welcome them to the ward, explain what was going to happen and reassure them.

A junior nurse poked her head round the curtain. 'There's a GP on the telephone—says he has to speak to the doctor in charge and it's urgent.'

Rosalind excused herself. 'Hello? This is Dr Grey.'

The man was angry. 'Dr Andrews here, Dr Grey. On Thursday last a Mr Ronald Able was discharged from your ward. His wife has been on the phone to me, asking about follow-up treatment. I know nothing of the case as I've had no letter and no notes. Would it be too much trouble to let me know what is happening?'

She kept her temper but, then, that had never been a problem for her. 'I'm very sorry, Dr Andrews. Could I phone you back in ten minutes when I've checked and found out what has happened?'

'Ten minutes? That'll be a miracle.' Dr Andrews rang off and Rosalind sighed.

Sister Talbot assured her that a letter had been sent, but managed to dig into a file and find the copy. 'These surgeries,' she muttered. 'They lose letters then phone and blame us.'

Rosalind knew this could be true, but decided to be diplomatic. 'Paperwork can go adrift,' she said.

She managed to get in touch with Dr Andrews with thirty seconds left of her ten-minute deadline, read him the letter and promised that a copy was on its way.

'About time,' Dr Andrews said ungraciously.

She had intended to walk through the ward, chat to each of the patients and try to get some idea of their medical histories. After she'd looked through the notes of the first two she was interrupted by a steely-faced Sister Talbot.

'Mrs Fellows's husband is on the phone, wanting to know how his wife is progressing. She had a colectomy last Wednesday. He's phoning from Aberdeen and doesn't intend to be fobbed off with a nurse. He insists on speaking to a doctor.'

The two of them hurried back to the sister's desk. 'Doesn't he realise you know ten times what I know?' Rosalind muttered.

Sister Talbot pointed to the phone and made to walk away. Rosalind covered the mouthpiece with her hand. 'Please don't go. I'm going to need you to tell me about this woman.' Slightly mollified, Sister Talbot waited by the desk.

'Dr Grey here.' It was a straightforward enquiry. Rosalind listened, then covered the mouthpiece and repeated the enquiry to the sister. Sister Talbot answered, then Rosalind relayed her answer word for word to Mr Fellows. Mr Fellows was satisfied.

'Sister could have answered your query, Mr Fellows,' Rosalind said finally. 'You didn't have to speak to a doctor.'

There was a snort at the other end of the line. 'I always go to the top. That way I get satisfaction.'

'Of course, Mr Fellows,' she said, and rang off. 'Sorry about that,' Rosalind said to Sister Talbot, and meant it. She believed nurses and doctors formed a partnership and neither could do without the other.

Sister Talbot shrugged. 'With my experience I ought to be used to ill-mannered relatives, but thanks for trying to put him right. Do you want to look round the ward some more?'

'Well, I was going to. Is there something else I should—?'

'Paperwork,' Sister said with a grim smile.

'There's a pile of letters, forms and case notes on the desk in the doctors' room. Some you can answer, some you file, some you keep for the consultant, some you throw in the bin. Just make sure each goes in the right pile.'

'Sounds fun,' Rosalind said dubiously.

In the afternoon a junior nurse called her. She was worried about Mr Gant. Earlier he'd refused his midday meal—which he never did. He wouldn't sit up in bed and wouldn't let her do her obs. He said his chest hurt.

'I'll come to have a look,' Rosalind said.

She pulled the curtains round Mr Gant's bed. Before she could look at his notes she'd decided that Mr Gant wasn't well. He seemed to be in pain.

'Hello, Mr Gant, I'm Dr Grey. I understand you didn't have your meal today?'

There was no answer from the bed, but a pair of dark eyes flicked open and focussed on her.

Rosalind eased down the sheet and reached for the pyjama top. 'If I could just listen to your chest, Mr Gant, I'd—'

The stethescope was slapped out of her hand. 'Don't come near me. Little chit of a girl. I want a real doctor, not some female.'

'I am a real doctor,' Rosalind said in some exasperation, 'and I'm trying to help you get better. Now, I need to—'

'I told you, I want a real doctor!' The old man's voice rose in a quavery shout.

Rosalind wasn't sure what to do. Should she wait till the old man calmed down? She thought he might need attention immediately but there was no way she could examine him by force.

'Now, then, Albert, are you causing trouble again?' A warm, and welcome male voice spoke behind her. She turned to see Mark, professional in white coat and dark trousers, silk shirt and a golden tie that echoed the colour of his hair.

'That's a real doctor,' grumbled a voice from the bed.

'We're both real doctors, Albert. Now behave and let the lady doctor look at you.'

Albert did. Rosalind examined him, but could hear nothing significant. Albert seemed willing enough to talk now, and said the pain had come on suddenly after breakfast. 'Just here, Doctor,' he said, pointing to his chest, 'like a fire inside me.'

Rosalind looked at his notes, then glanced at Mark. Mark gazed back imperturbably and waved at her to walk out of earshot. 'Diagnosis, Doctor?' he asked.

'Chest X-ray, obviously,' she said. 'Perhaps an ECG. But my diagnosis is simple acid reflux. Mr Gant has heartburn.'

'Not myocardial ischaemia? Or pulmonary embolus?'

'I doubt it, but we have to check, of course.'

'Good. Always well to be certain. But, like you, I'm ninety-nine per cent sure Mr Gant has simple indigestion.'

They stepped out into the corridor. 'I could have managed Mr Gant in time, you know,' she said. 'I was glad of your help, but I ought to be left to sort things out myself.'

'Ah. Tell me, Dr Grey, what advice would you give me if I had to conduct an intimate examination of a young, hysterical, drunken, teenage girl?'

The answer was obvious. 'Have someone female with

you as chaperon. Preferably a member of the family, otherwise a nurse.'

'Or lady doctor, such as yourself?'

'Yes, but…' She saw the point he was making. 'Mr Gant is a different case from your young female.'

'All cases are different, but if we help each other things get easier. Never turn up your nose at help, young Grey.'

'No, Doctor,' she said, mock-submissively. 'I shall certainly remember your very valuable lesson.'

'No cheek from you, woman. Remember my senior position.'

Sister Talbot, who was passing, looked surprised at this. He winked at her. 'Just disciplining the junior members, Sister.'

They went to the doctors' office, where she'd carefully arranged the mail. 'How d'you think you've done today?' he asked, tossing even more envelopes into the already full wastepaper basket.

'There's a couple of things I'd like to ask you about. I don't think I've made any great contribution to the health service, but I've coped.'

'If you've coped,' he said, 'then you've done well.'

Sister Talbot looked in. 'If you've a minute, Doctor…?'

'My life is made of minutes,' he murmured as he stood. 'Coming, Dr Grey?'

When she'd been a student there had usually been someone handy to offer advice. If she'd been allowed to perform some minor surgical process there'd always been an expert nearby to instruct or to take over if necessary. Now she was on her own.

She never had time to concentrate on just one task, get one thing exactly right. There was a constant avalanche of things she had to do, some important, some trivial, many that other people should have done but hadn't. And she loved it. But it was tiring.

After a week Rosalind was exhausted. On Saturday night she was on call, not officially on duty but expected to be available if necessary. And Saturday night was the night for surgical emergencies.

When she finally left the ward at five in the afternoon she had a quick meal, a shower and then lay on her bed to doze. She was now getting used to the idea that she should sleep whenever she could in case she didn't get another chance.

About ten the phone rang, but it wasn't from the ward. A voice said tersely, 'Can you get down to A and E? There's been a big accident and all hands are turning to. Your boss has asked for you.'

'Traffic accident?' she asked, reaching for her shoes.

'For a change, no. That old nightclub, Jake's Place. A balcony collapsed. Most people aren't seriously hurt, but a lot of them have been drinking—or taking drugs. Doesn't help things.'

Saturday night, she thought. She pulled on her white coat and hurried over to A and E. She knew the staff there quite well. Frequently surgical emergencies came into A and E and then were referred straight to her ward. She had to arrange the transfers.

She saw that the department was busier than usual, but not excessively so. It wasn't a full-scale emergency, for which there were set rules and procedures.

She asked a fast-moving nurse and was directed to a cubicle where she found Mark and Mike Gee, the A and

E consultant, leaning over the body of a moaning young girl. Rosalind could see a once vibrant red split skirt and black sparkly stockings. One shoe was gone, and skirt and stockings were covered in plaster dust and blood. The two men were engrossed with the girl's head and neck.

Mark looked up as a nurse hurried in, carrying X-rays, and fixed them to the illuminated panel. He saw Rosalind hovering behind and waved her over. The three of them looked at the X-rays.

'Fractured skull,' murmured Mike. 'Will you have her or is she a neurological case?'

Mark looked questioningly at Rosalind. After some thought she asked, 'May I see her eyes?'

Mark nodded. She leaned over and eased back the girl's eyelids. In one eye the pupil was tiny and in the other grossly dilated. 'There's pressure on the brain,' she said. 'Haematoma, intracerebral, extradural or subdural. Better get her a CAT scan and send for the neurological surgeon.'

'Good, I agree. And it's less work for us. I'll get Reception to phone the man on call.'

Mark turned to Rosalind. 'There are five cases in adjoining cubicles whom we might need to admit. We've done initial triage and I don't think there's anything life-threatening in any of them. Can you clerk them?'

'On my way,' said Rosalind.

She was given a male nurse to help her, Harry Dempsey. He was vast! She looked at his massively muscular forearms, cropped hair, thick neck and heavy shoulders. Then she looked at his gentle smile, and guessed he'd be a good nurse. 'Aren't you big?' she asked.

'I play rugby for the city and I work here Saturday nights,' he said. 'Being big helps in both jobs.'

First of all she looked in at all five patients to make sure nothing was seriously wrong. She also had a quick word with each. Mark had told her that nothing irritated a patient more than to be studied and ignored. Harry followed her closely. He obviously took his job as nurse/chaperon seriously.

'You've worked here longer than I have,' she told him. 'If you think I'm doing anything wrong don't hesitate to tell me.'

'You'll not do anything wrong,' he said encouragingly.

She had heard of Jake's Place, though she'd never been there. It was an old cinema which had been roughly converted into a rave palace for youngsters. The A and E department often had people brought from there after fights or drug overdoses.

She snapped on her first pair of rubber gloves. Of all places, A and E was where you never forgot your gloves.

Her first patient was called Stan Parks. 'What happened to you, then, Stan?' she asked, looking down at a young man in his Saturday best.

Stan was white-faced, but managed a grim smile. 'Terrible to be brought to hospital before I'm even drunk,' he croaked. 'And look! They've cut my new leather jacket!'

The jacket had indeed been cut away from Stan's left arm. In its place was a rough, blood-stained dressing, probably put there by the paramedics. With the scissors offered by Harry, she carefully cut away the dressing and eased it away from the arm. Fresh blood welled upwards, but not as quickly as it obviously had before.

'What happened, Stan?' she asked again, dabbing at the deep cut she had uncovered.

'Standing just below the balcony, enjoying myself, pint in my hand. The balcony fell and smashed the glass into my arm and knocked me over. When I got up my hand and arm were bleeding.'

'Hmm. Don't try too hard—but can you move your fingers?'

The effort was obviously painful and sweat appeared on his white brow. 'How's that?' he whispered.

It wasn't good. The broken glass had sliced down to the bone and nerves and tendons had been cut. There was no movement in his fingers.

'I think you've done some damage,' she said noncommitally. 'What do you do for a living, Stan?'

'I'm a carpenter.' Now he looked really alarmed. 'You can fix my hand, can't you, Doc? I need it for work.'

'I think we'd better admit you. You'll need to go into Theatre later. Can you remember if you've had a tetanus injection recently?'

He was certain he had when he'd started work, which was one good thing. She arranged for an X-ray to see if there were any fragments of glass left in the wound, and then said, 'Any other pains, cuts, anything?' It was all too easy to treat one injury and completely overlook another.

Stan had been knocked down, there was some bruising to his shoulder and a slight graze on his head, but she decided neither was serious. 'Just a few personal details, Stan,' she said, reaching for the pad. 'We'll get back to you when things get easier.' She decided to have a word with Mark. Stan might need a vascular surgeon or he might be seen by Mark himself but he wasn't an urgent case.

In the next cubicle a pretty but incredibly young girl was sobbing quietly. A dressing had been taped to her forehead. Someone had already ordered an X-ray of her head. Rosalind looked at it thoughtfully. There appeared to be no damage. When she examined the forehead she found it was little more than a large graze. Other than that, there were a number of minor cuts and bruises. The girl appeared to be more shocked than anything else. Rosalind sent Harry to fetch her a cup of sweet tea. This patient wasn't going to need a general anaesthetic.

'Diane, is it?' Rosalind asked comfortingly. 'Can you tell me what happened, Diane?'

'Me mam will kill me!'

'Your mam will be glad to see that you're all right. Where were you standing when the balcony fell?'

'Do you have to tell her? Can't I just go home?' Diane looked down at her dishevelled appearance and more tears appeared.

Rosalind looked at the childish face under the clumsily applied make-up. She thought she was getting the picture. 'How old are you, Diane?'

There were more tears, but Diane didn't dare lie. She was fourteen. 'I was supposed to be sleeping over at me mate's house. I said we were going to the pictures. Her mother doesn't mind her going out late 'cos she's older than me.'

'Is your friend wearing a red skirt? With black stockings that sparkle?'

'That's Ellen, all right. Can she come and talk to me?'

Rosalind decided to ignore the question. She'd seen Ellen with Mark and Mike and suspected that her problems were much worse than Diane's. 'I'm going to phone your mother and ask her to come and fetch you. What's her number, Diane?'

'But she'll go mad! I'm not allowed anywhere where there's drink, and specially not Jake's Place!'

'The phone number, Diane!'

Diane was too numb to argue further, and told them where her mother lived. Harry offered to ring and ask her to come.

The next two cases seemed reasonably straightforward. One man had a broken wrist—fortunately the X-rays showed a straightforward Colles' fracture with the typical dinner-fork deformity. After making absolutely sure that there were no other injuries, she took his details. He would have to go to Theatre to have the fracture reduced and then plastered.

Then she looked in on a man who was lying on a trolley with a loose dressing on his right hand. 'Do you know how long I've been waiting?' he snapped.

'Sorry. We are rather busy,' Rosalind said. 'Mr Stoll, is it? Could I see your hand?'

'I'm going to sue that Jake's Place. You may have to give evidence, Doctor.'

'Shall we see what's wrong first?'

'What's wrong is that my hand hurts like fury. And they won't even let me have a drink!'

She suspected that nothing was going to be good enough for this man. 'Can you tell me what happened, Mr Stoll?'

'I was sitting, enjoying my drink, when the balcony collapsed. Some oaf fell on top of me and knocked me down. I caught my hand on the edge of the table and I was winded. When I got my breath back I found that my hand was bleeding. The man who knocked me over wrapped his handkerchief round the cut and told me to hold it there tight. I trust the handkerchief was clean.'

Mr Stoll sat upright on the trolley, thrust his injured hand out and said, 'Here, take a look.'

She cut off the bandage. A great flap of skin had been pulled from the back of Mr Stoll's hand, revealing the tendons and flesh underneath. Mr Stoll took one glance and fainted.

'Shuts him up and saves giving him a local anaesthetic,' said Harry cheerfully. 'Shall I fetch the sutures, Doctor?'

The fifth case was different. Rosalind could tell by Harry's narrowed eyes and by the cautious way he stepped in front of her before she opened the curtain. This was the only person who hadn't replied when she'd first gone down the line, saying hello.

'This one might be a bit awkward,' he said. 'D'you think you ought to let a male doctor examine him?'

She pulled on a fresh pair of gloves. So far she thought she'd done a reasonable competent job on her own she wasn't going to call for help. 'I'll be all right,' she said.

This was an older man, more roughly dressed than the young people. 'The police brought him in,' Harry said. 'He's not from Jake's Place. He was found in the middle of the road. Apparently knocked down by a hit and run driver. Yet another RTA.'

The man was only half-awake, and didn't respond when Rosalind spoke to him. She didn't need to get too close to realise he stank of beer. 'We'd better get some clothes off him,' she told Harry. 'I can't examine him like that.'

'Leave it to me. It's a job I've done before.' Expertly Harry undressed the man then covered him with a sheet.

There didn't appear to be any major injuries to the body, apart from evidence of deep bruising to the abdomen. The man's breathing was stertorous and his face pale. It was when she took his blood pressure that she became alarmed. It was far, far too low. Why?

She felt the abdomen, it was hard, almost distended. 'I think he's bleeding internally,' she told Harry, 'This looks serious. It's likely to be a ruptured liver or spleen. We're going to need to do a laparotomy. Could you ask Mark or Mike to come in, please? I'll get some blood out of him for cross-matching.'

She guessed he was a drug addict as well as a drinker, and it was really hard to find a vein. But this was something she was good at, and eventually she located one and started to draw up the blood. The man moaned and muttered something. 'Soon be finished,' Rosalind said brightly.

It was completely unexpected. Suddenly the man went mad! His free arm scythed across the trolley, smashing into her shoulder and knocking her against the table that held her instruments. The table crashed over with a jangle of falling glass and metal. She fell heavily, painfully jarring her back, the breath crushed out of her. For a moment she couldn't move.

It all seemed to happen in slow motion. The man rolled over and was above her. 'I stick my own needles in, thank you,' he snarled. 'See how you like it.' He snatched the blood-filled syringe from her powerless hand and before she could do anything to stop him he had jammed it deep into her arm. It hurt. His thumb found the plunger and she *saw* the blood level diminish.

Then the curtain was ripped aside and she saw Harry effortlessly lifting the man away from her. Even in her fright she noticed how carefully he did it. .

With a loud crack the syringe fell to the floor. It had been full but was now half-empty.

'Rosalind, are you all right? Don't get up, just lie there a minute.' It was Mark, his usually confident voice for once sounding strained. He knelt by her side and his hands checked her head and limbs.

'I'm all right, just shocked,' she muttered. 'Let me get up.'

'I'll keep an eye on this one if you want to take Dr Grey out,' Harry said from behind them. 'He won't cause me any trouble.'

'Is there trouble here?' It seemed that everyone was trying to get into her cubicle. This time it was Mike, the A and E consultant. He looked at the patient, now quiet under Mike's gaze. 'That's Lennie Shore,' he said. 'I should have been told he was here.'

'You know him?' Mark asked.

'Very well, I'm afraid. He's got AIDS.'

'He's just injected half a syringe of his blood into me,' Rosalind said.

CHAPTER FIVE

MARK took her to the doctors' rest room, and Rosalind sat there as he pulled off her gloves and rolled up her sleeve. The puncture mark where the syringe had gone in was ragged and blood was running down her arm. He placed a bowl under the small wound and told her to squeeze her arm with the other hand.

'Primitive medicine,' he said with a wry smile. 'We're bleeding you. But we're still going to stick a needle in a vein as we're going to need some blood for the lab. Now, do you hurt anywhere else?'

'I'm fine,' she reassured him. 'Just a bit shocked. I'll be able to get back to work in a minute.'

'No question of that. Things are under control now. In a minute I'll see you back home.'

'But I want to—'

'Learn to do as you're told, young Grey!' There was a touch of anger in the half-mocking tone. 'I've sent for my SHO and Mike thinks he can do without us now. We're both off duty.'

There was a knock on the door and Harry peered round. His amiable face was concerned. 'Dr Gee sent this, 'he said to Mark, and placed a packet on the table. Then he turned to look at her. 'Are you all right, Dr Grey? You know, I feel terrible. I never should have left you. I thought he might be trouble.'

'I'm fine, Harry,' she said hesitantly. 'Er, there's one thing, though…'

He knew what was worrying her. 'I've already made my report to Dr Gee. I shan't mention the incident to anyone else.'

'Thanks, Harry.' The last thing she wanted was to be talked about. She could do without the curiosity and the sympathy. Harry walked out. Mark brought her coffee, and she noticed him stir three teaspoons of sugar into it. It would taste vile but she knew it was what her shocked body needed. Then he unwrapped the packet Mike had brought.

'Pill time, Rosalind. It's AZT—azathioprine, an immunosuppressive drug. You're to continue taking these for the next three months. I don't like using cytotoxic drugs, but chemotherapy is the best thing for you now.' He frowned. 'You know they're going to make you feel bad?'

'I know,' she said briefly, 'but I can manage.'

She could see his absorbed blue eyes and the determined curve of his lips. He caught her looking at him, and he looked straight back. For a moment she caught a flash of an emotion she didn't recognise. It was pain or even terror, but it was gone swiftly and she thought she'd imagined it.

'You know what's happened?'

His voice was calm, neutral. Hers was equally controlled. 'I've just taken a dose of a cytotoxic drug. It is designed to combat the effects of the HIV virus. It might or might not work.'

She went on. 'In my body I've now got the body fluids of a man who has AIDS. I could be infected with HIV, but it will be impossible to tell with any certainty for three months.'

'Impressive, Rosalind. You've got the lecture memorised word for word. But I'm afraid that knowing something is not the same as experiencing it.' He sat silently for a moment, then said, 'Hospital policy is that all cases like this be referred to one man. Fortunately, that man is Mike and he already knows about you. He'll want to arrange counselling for you.'

'I don't need counselling,' she said. 'I'm far too busy.'

'Rosalind,' he asked, 'do you know how lonely you're going to feel?'

From somewhere she could hear a tinny sound. She looked around and her gaze dropped to her coffee-mug. She was holding it against the arm of her chair but her hand was trembling, shaking so much that the mug was rattling against the metal arm and coffee was spilling onto the floor. Mark reached over and took it from her.

It's only nervous reaction, she told herself. A perfectly natural thing to happen. Just the body reacting against stress. But she knew it wasn't true. She was terrified.

Mark took away the blood and put a dressing on the puncture. Then he lifted her bodily. The strength seemed to have left her legs. He carried her to a couch in the corner of the room and sat her there, before sitting next to her.

He took off his white coat and put his arm round her. She leaned into his shoulder, feeling the muscles of his chest, shoulder and arm. Pectorals, deltoid, biceps, she told herself hysterically. But it was warm and comfortable there. She could feel the heat of his body, even the faint smell of cologne. She didn't feel better but she felt less bad.

'Good medical practice,' she said after a while, when she thought she could talk without her voice betraying her. 'In cases of shock the patient is to be kept warm, comforted and reassured.'

'All available on the National Health,' he informed her. He reached over and stroked her hair. 'You and your sisters have beautiful hair,' he said. 'It's both the same and it's different, but it's all beautiful.'

She liked having her hair stroked. It was restful. Lying here with Mark beside her, she could convince herself that she had no troubles, that all was well…

It was time to move. The period of emotion was over. She was Rosalind Grey, now a doctor, known for being hard-headed, unemotional, in charge of her own feelings. There was no problem she couldn't face.

She stood, walked to the little sink and rinsed her face. He remained sitting, his expression perfectly blank. 'Haven't you any work to do?' she asked.

'Thank you for that resounding vote of confidence in my charms and presence,' he said drily.

She gestured impatiently. 'You know what I mean. I'm…I'm glad you were here but there's an emergency and—'

'The emergency is largely over. However, as I told you, I've sent for my SHO so neither you nor I are needed here now.'

He looked at his watch. 'It's still quite early. I think you should phone one or both of your sisters, tell them what has happened and go to stay with one for the night.'

'No.' She was definite. 'They have problems of their own— they don't need mine. For a start, Lisa's having a baby in three months.'

'Rosalind, you need to confide in someone. Your sis-

ters would confide in you. And they would—they will—
be angry if you don't tell them and they find out later.'

She was still assertive. 'I'm not my sisters, and I've
never unloaded my problems on them.'

'You've never had a problem like this before.'

'I know that,' she said bleakly, 'but, for me, sharing
a problem would make it harder to bear. I can carry my
own burden. I think.'

She must still be in shock. She hadn't meant to add
those last two words, to reveal her own doubt. She knew
he'd noticed them but he didn't comment.

'I don't think you should spend the night by yourself,
but the choice is yours. I'll walk you over to your room,
and I've got a sedative here for you. Go straight to bed.
We'll talk further in the morning.'

She had to be forthright. 'I'm not going to change my
mind, you know.'

'I do know, and I'm not going to change mine. You
do need some kind of counselling. It can provide comfort that we doctors can't provide.'

She tried to be light-hearted. 'I just had an unfortunate
incident. One in every ten hospital workers gets attacked
by a patient. I'm one of those one in ten.'

'In this case, that attack might be a death sentence.'

He was harder than she had realised. To hear it said
so bluntly shocked her. For the first time in fourteen
years she felt tears come to her eyes. She hadn't cried
since she was nine. 'I don't cry,' she said, forcing her
voice to stay calm.

He offered her a handkerchief. 'Of course not. Use
this to wipe the grit out of your eye, then I'll walk you
over to the residency.'

'But I ought to—'

'Just do as you're told.' There was a bite in his voice she hadn't heard before. 'Now I need a sample of blood. Roll up your sleeve.'

After the controlled chaos of the A and E department the hospital grounds were strangely peaceful. They paced together, hearing the distant sounds of traffic and voices but unaffected by them. Against the dark sky reared the tall surgical block, a patchwork of lighted windows. She could see stars above it.

'So don't tell your family if you don't want to,' he said, 'though I think that's what families are for. I haven't got a family—it makes me an expert.'

No family? She decided to ask him about it later.

He went on, 'For the moment I'll keep things quiet as that's what you want. But if I feel it necessary I'll tell who I like.'

'What about medical confidentiality?' she asked, with some show of spirit.

It was dark, but she knew he was grinning by the tone of his voice.

He slapped her on the shoulder. 'I can say what I like, I'm not your doctor. If anything, you're mine. Now there must, of course, be no danger to our patients. Mike will advise you on that, and he'll also inform me. So far there's no need for you to worry. You'll have to take a blood test every month and I'll monitor the results.'

'I'd like that.'

'And if you refuse counselling then you'll have to come and talk to me. I've always fancied myself as a psychoanalyst. You can come and lie on my couch and tell me things. I'll grow a beard again and cultivate a Viennese accent.'

'I'm not coming if you've got a beard.'

'All right. We'll pass on the beard.'

They had now reached the front steps of the residency. He gave her a foil sachet. 'I'm usually against drugs for doctors, but take this sedative tonight. It's five mils of valium.'

'I'll take it,' she said, and he knew she meant it.

'"My family hug a lot,"' he quoted, and hugged her. She liked it.

As she walked upstairs she realised she was glad Mark was looking after her. Not that she needed looking after, of course, but she'd be glad of Mark's help. He inspired confidence. She looked at the sedative he'd given her. She had intended to flush it down the toilet but instead, she fetched a glass of water and swallowed it.

Next morning there was a phone call while Rosalind was still in bed. She knew who it would be. 'Good morning,' a drowsy voice said. 'Did you sleep well?'

'Very well at first,' she told him truthfully, 'but I woke early this morning and stayed awake.'

'Well, it was only a mild sedative.'

'In fact, by the sound of your voice, I slept a lot better than you did.'

'Ah. We had an emergency case last night. The SHO and I had to operate.'

She was getting to know him. There was an inflection in his voice that told her certain things. 'Anything to do with the case I was dealing with?' she asked. She was pleased that her voice remained firm.

'Yes. Your suspicions were correct. Lennie Shore had massive bleeding into the spleen. It wasn't the best time to operate but we had no choice. We did a splenectomy but he couldn't stand the shock and died an hour after we'd got him back on the ward.'

'I'm sorry,' she said, and she was.

'He didn't have much future,' Mark said flatly. 'Anyway, I'm going to bed now. Have you changed your mind about confiding in anyone?'

'No.'

'Now, that is surprising,' he said sardonically. 'Well, the best prescription for you is work. I know you're supposed to be off but get into the ward and make yourself useful. We admitted another man last night—technically for observation. Name of Hallows. Clerk him and have a poke around. See if you can decide what's wrong with him. I'm sure I don't know.'

'I'll bet you don't,' she said.

Mr Hallows turned out to be an apparently fit, forty-year-old man who had been admitted for haematemesis—he had suddenly vomited blood. There had been no shock and blood pressure and pulse were within acceptable limits so, after a transfusion, he had been left until morning. The nursing staff checked on him hourly. Now it was Rosalind's task to clerk him and to try to find some reason for the sudden attack.

Mr Hallows was baffled. He had never vomited blood before. He had no history of gastrointestinal illness. He was not on any drugs that might produce ulcers. When Rosalind examined him she could find no indication of intra-abdominal pathology, no mass or tenderness.

'I feel fine now,' he told Rosalind. 'Perhaps I should go home.'

'Not a good idea,' she said. 'I think I'll send you for an endoscopy. They'll have a look round and see what they can find.'

She still marvelled at the latest fibre-optic endoscope. The idea of sending a flexible tube into a man's stomach and looking at what was inside was magic. It made diagnosis so much easier.

In the afternoon she was sitting in the doctors' room, writing up more reports, when Mark looked round the door. 'The pen is mightier than the scalpel,' he said. 'Just think of the medicine you could practise if you weren't constantly writing.'

'A doctor I know said never get behind in your paperwork,' she told him. 'Why are you here on a Sunday?'

'Can't keep away from you. And I'm interested in the man I admitted—oh, this morning.'

'He's got a peptic ulcer,' she said. 'I sent him for a fibre-optic endoscopy and they found the ulcer. Mark, he'd had no previous history whatsover. No pain, no bleeding, no discomfort.'

Mark nodded. 'It's very unusual but it's not unheard of,' he said. 'What do we do now?'

'Surgical intervention, I suppose,' she said. 'Then advice on changing his lifestyle. I can't make the decision, though.'

He looked at her with respect. 'Well, we'll go to look at him in a minute, but I suspect you're right. Well done, young Grey. You can help me operate.' He shut the door firmly behind him and said, with a casualness she didn't believe, 'And how are you, Rosalind?'

'Your prescription was right, Doctor. All I needed was work.'

His face was expressionless. 'Come to me when you need a repeat prescription.'

*   *   *

That evening she went to Lisa's for supper. She played with Jack and Holly and told Holly how much she'd enjoyed her party, especially the choice of records.

'I did consider becoming a DJ in time,' Holly told her, 'but I think I'd rather be a doctor.'

'It's a difficult choice,' Rosalind told her. For once she wondered if a life in medicine was as wonderful as some people thought. In fact, as *she'd* always thought.

She put the children to bed then settled in the living room with Lisa and Alex. Alex put his arm round his wife as he sat beside her on the couch. That's nice, Rosalind thought. For a moment she wished she had someone who would do that to her.

'So, how's being a houseman?' Alex asked her cheerfully. 'I don't really want to know—it's just an excuse for me to tell you how things were harder in my day.'

Lisa pushed her husband. 'Let her talk,' she scolded.

'I like it,' Rosalind said, 'but so far it's been a bit too much like fire-fighting. There's always something else to do so I don't have time to get really interested in a patient or a case. Different from when I was a student.'

Alex nodded. 'It's a common complaint. But you'll learn to deal with the volume of work and then you'll be able to concentrate more on your patients. How're you getting on with Mark Harrison?'

She glanced at him quickly, but it seemed an innocent question. 'Very well,' she said carefully. 'He's helpful— a very good teacher. I'm learning a lot from him.'

'Doesn't push you too hard? Doesn't think you can go for days without sleep?'

'No. He's reasonable that way.'

Alex pulled at his ear. 'He's changed. When he first came to the university hospital he was an absolute fanatic for work. Didn't seem to sleep at all—and that's among people who don't sleep much anyhow. He was obsessive. And then he went off to the South Seas, where you met him, and he'd lost the obsession when he came back.'

'Probably made him a better doctor,' Rosalind said.

'I like him,' Lisa chipped in. 'I think he's the second-best-looking man in the hospital.' She kissed her husband on the cheek.

I wish I could have someone whom I could just kiss on the cheek when I wanted, Rosalind thought. Sisters are fine—but they're not the same.

At the end of her second week Rosalind was getting into the swing of things. Work was as never ending and as tiring as ever. Then Mark asked her if she'd like to do some practical work for him. 'Surgeons use scalpels,' he told her. 'You'd better get some practice in.'

It was day case surgery, and would only need local anaesthetics. Five patients came in to have minor swellings and cysts removed. As the patient was conscious it was more than a simple excision—the patient had to be kept calm. Even though there was no pain, she knew that the hospital surroundings frightened many people.

'People, not cases,' Mark whispered to her. 'Perform the operation but keep them happy as well.'

The first case was a simple sebaceous cyst. Not a cyst, she corrected herself. It was Mrs Landon who had a sebaceous cyst on her head. As Mark looked on approvingly she talked to the woman for a while, explaining what was happening and how it would soon be over. Then she began.

First she infiltrated the skin surrounding the cyst with

lignocaine. Then she incised the skin, used artery forceps to ease between the skin and the cyst. The cyst was lifted out. It was then easy to suture, picking up the floor of the cyst with each stitch.

'All done,' she said to Mrs Landon. 'You can have the stitches taken out in a week.'

Mrs Landon looked surprised. 'Is that all? If I'd known, I'd have had it done years ago.'

Rosalind decided she liked this work.

She didn't see much of her co-housemen, Alison and Eric. Alison seemed even more withdrawn but was coping with the work, but Eric was angry.

At the beginning of one of her shifts Rosalind found a pile of forms on the doctors' desk which he should have completed. He'd left them. Eric didn't live in the residency. He'd recently got married and had a tiny flat near the hospital. Since she knew he'd only just have got home she phoned him.

'Leave them,' Eric said angrily. 'We're slaves, not real doctors. Nurses could fill in those forms.'

'But, Eric—'

'I said leave them! Throw them in the bin for all I care.' He slammed down the receiver.

Rosalind sighed and reached for the first form. She could probably fit them in. She knew Eric's new wife had a nine to five job and didn't understand what hospital work was like.

'Coping?' Mark asked three days later as he sauntered onto the ward.

Rosalind stood upright from the patient whose blood

pressure she'd been taking. 'Course I'm coping,' she said, rubbing her aching back. 'I always cope.'

She smiled down at her patient. 'That's fine, Mrs Mellon. We won't be bothering you any more.'

'Let's go into the doctors' room,' Mark suggested. 'You look as if you need a rest.'

When she flopped down on a chair in their little room he went to pour her a coffee. Giving it to her, he said, 'You're tired. Don't you have enough to do, without covering for other people, too?'

She felt angry. 'Don't play tricks with me,' she snapped. 'If you've anything to say, say it.'

He was apparently unmoved by her anger. 'You've been carrying Eric Hart. Most of the paperwork that should have come from him has been completed by you.'

'What does it matter if it gets done?'

'It matters to you, to Eric and to the patients he's ultimately in charge of. You're doing him no favours by carrying him. He'll start to make mistakes then he'll think it's someone else's fault. He has to be responsible to himself, Rosalind.'

'But he's just got married and—'

'I know about his marriage—he told me—but this is something he has to sort out. I'm going to have a word with him. Promise me you won't do any more of his work?'

'Promise *me* you'll be kind to him.'

He looked hurt. 'Of course I'll be kind to him. Kindness is my middle name. Marcus Kindness Aloysius Harrison. Just worry about yourself, young Grey.' He turned to go. 'Oh, one more thing. You've got tomorrow off. Any special plans?'

'I've got washing to do,' she told him. 'There's some reading up I'd like to get through and I need to do some shopping. Then I might visit Emily or Lisa and—'

She looked up to see him grinning at her. 'All right,' she said, 'I'll probably sleep for most of the day.'

'Good. After your sleep I'd like you to come to tea.'

She looked at him uncertainly. 'Tea?'

'Dainty stuff in teacups. A mild stimulant because of its caffeine content. More sophisticated men than me invite young ladies to dinner. I'm common, I'm inviting you to tea. We need to talk.'

'All right,' she said. 'I'm looking forward to it.'

'Good. Nothing formal, you're only coming for an hour or so. We will be unchaperoned but, since I'm old enough to be your father, that's all right.'

'You're not old enough to be my father!'

'Ten years older. And there are cases in—'

'Don't tell me, I don't want to know.'

She looked at his amiable smiling face. Just tea, she thought. Did she feel just a touch disappointed?

Nothing formal, he had said, so she decided to go in jeans and sweater. Then she got irritated with herself when she realised how long she'd spent, choosing what to wear. She'd picked a dark pair of jeans and a deep green top that went well with her eyes.

'I live in Gingerbread Hall,' he'd said, and she'd thought he was joking as usual. But when she found his home she realised the name was very apt. Blazes Hospital site was vast. Her bit of the hospital was modern, but there were older, red-brick bits and here and there remnants of the original Blazes Grange. Gingerbread Hall was one.

It had once been a gardener's cottage or something like that. It was a tiny building with ornamental brickwork, leaded, coloured windows and fantastic woodwork. She could imagine someone from a fairy story living here. Was Mark from a fairy story?

She lifted an elaborate brass knocker. It hit the door with a boom.

On the island she'd seen him in shorts and shirt, but he'd been more formally dressed since then. Now he answered the door in T-shirt and trousers, his feet bare. 'Welcome to Gingerbread Hall,' he said. 'Do come in.'

He'd put on a little weight since she'd seen him on the island, but there was still no fat on him. His muscles were still lean and corded. Unusually for a blond man, he was still tanned.

As she stepped inside he warned her, 'If you eat the walls then I'll eat you.'

'You're not a witch,' she scoffed. 'According to my picture book, the witch is old and bent and knobbly.'

'I'm sorry. I shall work on acquiring knobbles. But come in, anyway.'

She looked around. 'It *is* just like a doll's house. Not that I ever played with dolls.'

'Now, how might I have guessed that?' he asked.

Inside there was just one room on the ground floor, with a kitchen annexe at the back. The decorations were like those outside, a riot of convoluted plasterwork and woodwork. But it had been painted simply. Walls and ceiling were plain white and the fitted carpet a dark fawn. All the furniture and woodwork was varnished clear pine. There was just one touch of colour, a large couch which had been upholstered in red leather.

'How did you get this place?' she asked.

He shrugged. 'The hospital bursar wasn't sure what to do with it. I said I'd like it 'cos I wanted to live on site. I paid for the alterations, the decorations and the furniture. When I leave, the hospital will give it to the National Trust and men in grey suits will take conducted tours. Would you like to look around?'

She most certainly would. 'What else is there?' she asked.

'We can tour the kitchen and you can admire my freezer. Then there's upstairs. I think I've made the bed.' He led her to the back of the room, where an open staircase led upwards.

Upstairs there was simply a bathroom and a bedroom. The decorations were the same as on the ground floor. She remembered his house on the island and wasn't surprised at how both were spartan.

'No pictures,' she said when they were back in the living room. 'No ornaments, not even a photograph of the island.'

Mark shook his head. 'I don't want possessions. And I don't need photographs to remember.'

They sat, she on the couch and he on the floor with his back against the fireplace edge. It was obviously a favourite place for him.

Suddenly Rosalind remembered what Will had said about him. That he was a womaniser. What had he had in mind when he'd invited her here? She'd not thought about the accusation much as it was quite at odds with the way she found him. She decided she was perfectly comfortable. She knew she'd be safe.

She remembered something else. 'You said you had no family,' she said. 'Is that why you have no photographs?'

'When I told you that I thought you had enough problems of your own to think about,' he said. 'I'm surprised you remembered.'

'Well, I did. Sometimes you…intrigue me.

'It's a simple story. I was an only child. My father was a soldier, killed in one of those little wars we forget about. I was at boarding school and my mother died of cancer when I was sixteen. There's a couple of relatives I send Christmas cards to in Australia, but that's all.'

'That's terrible. I'm mean, I couldn't manage without my family. We—'

'Help each other and confide in each other,' Mark said softly. 'Sometimes I envy you, Rosalind, I really do.'

'You tricked me,' she cried. 'You're cunning. But I still don't want to tell them.'

'Couldn't stand the sympathy?' he suggested. 'Things are easier to bear on your own?'

'Yes. How did you know that?'

'I've been on my own a lot,' he said. 'I suppose I can guess. Now, how are you coping with your problem?'

'I'm coping,' Rosalind said flatly. 'Sometimes the AZT makes me feel bad but I know the odds against me being infected are reasonably high. I've a better chance then a lot of the people who pass through the ward. But every morning I remind myself. I tell myself that in a few weeks I might find I'm HIV positive and there's nothing I can do about it.'

'Facing up to the problem makes it go away?'

'No. Not go away. I can manage it and even be happy—a bit.'

'If you're tough, that's the best way,' he said. Something about the way he spoke and the sudden bleak look on his face made her think that he was remembering something himself. Perhaps his childhood. But the expression had only been a fleeting one.

He reached over to touch her on the leg. There was an obvious change of mood. 'Tell me about your father. Alex said something about South America, and that he's coming home soon.'

Her face lit up. 'Yes, isn't it great! Two of his daughters have got married and he couldn't manage to get home. And I know he'd have loved to. He brought us all up, but as soon as I got into medical school he set off, wandering. He said we should be on our own for a few years. But I know he was sad to miss the weddings.'

'He's got one daughter left,' Mark pointed out.

'If that's a subtle question, it's not very subtle. As it says in Jane Austen, I have no ideas for matrimony at the present.'

He sniffed. 'Eventually, *everybody* gets married in Jane Austen. If they're good, that is.'

Rosalind decided to change the subject. 'My father was kidnapped by guerillas, but they got to like him and he decided to stay with them. He's a teacher, you know.'

He nodded, and the conversation lapsed. She felt quite comfortable, sitting there with him. Sometimes he could be a restful man. She didn't need to talk to feel at home with him.

'I invited you to tea,' he said. 'It's not really dainty, but it's how I like it. Come and sit down.' He sat her at a small table and, with a flourish, spread a blue tablecloth on it. 'We've dined together in the tropics,' he said, 'but that was always Matilda's cooking. Now it's up to me.'

Mark fetched a teatray, with a big traditional earthenware pot. 'Teabags are OK,' he told her, 'but I prefer the real thing.'

Then he fetched another tray. She blinked. 'Not exactly dainty cucumber sandwiches, are they?' she asked.

He looked down proudly. 'The sandwich is a British invention. It represents perfection to equal anything that French or Chinese cuisine can come up with. D'you know the French make sandwiches without butter? Ludicrous. I make excellent sandwiches. And there is some cucumber in there. Among other things.'

Dubiously, Rosalind picked up one of his sandwiches. It needed two hands to stop bits falling out. 'My father would have called this a doorstop,' she mumbled, and then bit into it. Her eyes opened wide. She'd never had a sandwich like it.

For a start, the bread was perfect. There was thick butter, the moistest of ham and an array of salad. Spread over all was a delicate dressing.

'Good, isn't it?' he asked smugly. 'I'll pour you some tea now.'

She had two sandwiches, one with white bread and one with brown. He had the same. She just couldn't manage another so he took them away and fetched a plate of fruit. 'I'll freeze the sandwiches,' he said. 'We bachelors learn tricks like that.'

They took their second cup of tea back to the couch. 'I really enjoyed that,' she said. 'It was…different.'

He bowed. 'A tiny thank you for your party. And I'm pleased to try out my counselling skills.'

'Counselling?' she asked in surprise. 'What about the couch and the Viennese accent?'

'Well, I have to begin somewhere. And—' His bleeper went. He checked it, then went over to the phone.

'Don't worry, Eric... Yes, put a drip up and watch her... I'll be over in ten minutes... No, you were right to call.'

He turned to her and said ruefully. 'It's Eric. We had a talk, but he's still not quite confident enough. You wouldn't have called me out for this, but I'd better get over. Sorry, young Grey, I'm throwing you out. Be grateful that you've had your tea.'

'I told you that I enjoyed it.'

'Will you come again?'

'I'd like to. And if you're asking if it helped me then, yes, it did. You're a better doctor than you pretend, aren't you, Dr Harrison?'

Mark looked at her, bewildered. 'Have I been complimented or insulted?'

'I leave you to decide. Will you hug me?'

He did. Again there was that remembered feeling of warmth and comfort. But there was also something else. She knew he felt it, too. There was reluctance in the way he pushed her away. 'You must go, young Grey.' He kissed her on the cheek. 'Keep fighting.'

Rosalind had enjoyed herself. As she walked back through the hospital grounds she realised she felt better than she had done in days. She had needed a non-serious interlude and Mark had provided it. It struck her that he'd done it on purpose. He was a more subtle man than she'd realised. She couldn't think of anyone whose company she enjoyed more.

Perhaps that made him a dangerous man.

CHAPTER SIX

ROSALIND'S good humour lasted through the next morning. First she had a quick word with Sister Talbot about the patients. There was nothing that demanded her attention but Mrs Kent… Sister shook her head. Mrs Kent was being kept comfortable. That was all that could be done for her. Rosalind went to look, anyway.

There were the bloods to do, assorted drugs to prescribe and reports to write. But she'd been working for nearly a month now and was learning how to cope with pressure. There were tasks she could delegate to a senior student or the nurses. She learned how to triage—what was urgent, what could wait.

At midmorning she had managed to grab a cup of coffee when Sister appeared. 'Rosalind, Mrs Kent has just died.'

'I'll come,' said Rosalind. She knew Sister was right, but only a doctor could certify death.

'I'll prepare her a bit,' Sister said. 'Her husband always comes about this time. You'll have to tell him, Rosalind.'

She would. It was a task she'd never had before. She'd spoken to Mr Kent several times. Indeed, she'd tried to tell him that things didn't look good for his wife. He was a kindly man, but he just didn't want to listen.

'I've every faith in the hospital, Doctor,' he had said. 'I know you'll help her pull through.'

She'd heard of this determination not to face facts

before. Some relatives just wouldn't—or couldn't—listen to bad news. She wondered how she should tell Mr Kent. Whatever, it was her responsibility, and it was part of her job to do it to cause as little pain as possible. She remembered Mark's advice. Medicine was an art as well as a science.

A nurse warned Rosalind that Mr Kent had just stepped out of the lift, and Rosalind went to intercept him. 'Would you like to come to my room, Mr Kent?'

He was a thin, stooped man of about sixty-five. At first he said nothing when she spoke to him, but when the tired eyes focussed on her she guessed he already knew what she had to say.

'When was it?' he asked quietly.

She hadn't wanted this to happen in the corridor, with nurses and patients walking past and looking at them curiously. But she had to answer his question.

'About half an hour ago. We tried to phone you but there was no reply. It was peaceful, Mr Kent. She felt no pain. Please come in here.'

A nurse slipped into the doctors' room with tea for him. 'Is there anyone you'd like me to phone?' she asked.

'Thank you, no. If I could have a minute to collect myself, then I'd like to see her. I'm sorry to be so much trouble.'

'You're no trouble, Mr Kent. We're only sorry…well, we're sorry.' She stood.

'You don't have to go,' he said, alarmed. 'In fact, if you could stay…'

So she sat again.

Mark came in briefly to pick up some case notes an hour later, and asked Rosalind how things were going. She told him about Mr Kent. 'He'd never admit that she was seriously ill, Mark, and yet he knew at once that she was dead.'

Mark put his arm round her shoulders. 'People are strange, Rosalind. Every doctor should have that carved on his or her desk. Diseases are straightforward, but people are strange.'

It was a peculiar way of putting things, but she knew he was right.

It had been the first death certificate Rosalind had ever signed. Not much of a milestone, she thought to herself, and decided to get out of the ward at lunchtime. Unusually for her, she went over to the canteen. Perhaps someone she knew would be there. She needed company.

She collected herself a salad and looked around. She saw Alison, who waved at her vigorously. She hoped Alison would be good company.

Alison was smiling, vivacious, eager to talk. And Rosalind had thought she was unhappy. But Alison had questions to ask. 'What's this about you and our wonderful Mark, then?' she asked, mock-cheerfully.

Rosalind desperately tried to keep a straight face. 'What's what, then?' she asked carelessly.

'You were seen, coming out of his little house. This is the hospital, luvvie, you can't keep anything secret.'

Rosalind knew that this was largely true. All hospital staff loved to gossip, but there was still one secret she held and she hoped that wasn't general knowledge. But about Mark…

'He's a friend of the family,' she mumbled. 'I just

called in and had a cup of tea with him. He's years older than me.'

'Well, I wouldn't care,' Alison said, energetically demolishing her plate of pie and chips. 'Good luck to you. I don't think you'll get anywhere, though.'

'I'm not trying to *get anywhere*,' Rosalind said, irritated.

But Alison was not in the mood for recognising subtle mood changes. 'You might as well know,' she said. 'I got fed up with moping about, thinking about Harold and how I'd wasted so much of my time on him. And this job's so demanding I never meet anyone nice. So I tried to get Mark to take me out. I told him I had tickets for that rock concert, and would he like to go with me? He was gentle, but he told me to find someone my own age to go with. So I upped and told him that it wasn't the concert I wanted, it was him.'

'You did what?' Rosalind was shocked by the intensity of emotions this confession aroused in her. How could Alison do such a thing? Somehow she managed to keep her feelings under control and pretend that she was concerned solely for her friend. Not that the miserable girl opposite her was bothered about anything but herself.

Alison laid down her knife and fork. 'I gave it to him straight—whatever he wanted he could have.' She pushed her plate away, her shoulders shaking. 'He didn't want me.'

In spite of the surprises she'd just had, Rosalind decided she had to be helpful. 'Look,' she said, 'you've had a shock, losing Harold. You were together a long time, and this new job doesn't make things any easier.

You're under stress. Hell, we're all under stress. Here, blow your nose.' She offered a tissue.

Alison took it and went on, 'He was so good to me. Couldn't have been nicer. He said he liked me a lot, he even fancied me. But he thought of himself as my teacher. And he didn't approve of senior medical staff taking advantage of junior staff. So now I fancy him more than ever because I know it's pointless.'

'He sounds very conscientious,' Rosalind said thoughtfully, 'but I always thought he was.'

Alison left shortly afterwards. Rosalind fetched herself a coffee and sat alone, reflecting. She had to sort out her own feelings.

Why had she felt that jolt of primitive rage when Alison had told her sad little story? It wasn't anger at Mark—he appeared to have acted well. With something like horror, Rosalind managed to define the emotion she had felt. It was jealousy. She didn't want him with other women. She might try to fool herself that Mark was nothing but a good family friend, but he was more than that. He was turning into something very special.

Now what do I do? she asked herself.

She had forgotten about hospital gossip. As a student she hadn't mixed too much—and the hospital and university had tended to be distinct entities. But Blazes was a hothouse of gossip.

She was unpleasantly reminded of this three days later when she went out with Will. She hadn't seen him for a while as he'd been on a course in London.

He called and invited her to dinner in Chez Marcus, a French restaurant in the centre of town, much frequented by senior medical staff. She noticed the way he looked around as they were shown to their seats. Will liked to see and be seen.

For most of the meal he talked about the course he'd been on. That suited her fine. Although she had no intention of becoming an anaesthetist, she liked to keep in touch with recent developments. And Will liked to talk.

Then, just as they were starting their ice cream, Will asked sharply, 'What's this I hear about you seeing Mark Harrison?'

He should have been warned by the level gaze she gave him— he wasn't. 'He's my specialist registrar,' she said. 'I have to see a lot of him.'

'You know what I mean. You were seen coming out of that ridiculous little house of his.'

'I like the house,' she said thinly, 'and I visit who I like.'

Will realised he had said the wrong thing. 'Of course you do, my dear.' He reached over to clasp her hand. She carefully disengaged it.

'I was just thinking about you,' he went on. 'You know the man has a bit of a reputation.'

'So you say. The only reputation I've heard is of him being a very good teacher and doctor.'

Will didn't like to be contradicted. 'He might be discreet but he's a ladies' man. He won't settle down to a relationship and I think that's wrong. He's been seen taking out a sister from Ward 29. There was Lesley Randall, who's head of radiography. Why, he's even taken out my boss.'

'Mary-Lou Day?' Rosalind asked, surprised. Mary-Lou was a visiting American consultant anaesthetist, very attractive and rather formidable.

'Mary-Lou,' Will confirmed.

Rosalind wasn't quite sure what she felt. She knew Will's story would be true. He delighted in gossip but always took pains to be accurate. 'They're all older women,' she said after a while. 'And I suspect, all very capable of taking care of themselves. I can't see him taking an interest in someone young like me.'

'You never know,' Will said primly. 'Better not give him the chance. Now, do I take it that you won't be going to his house again?'

'You take it that I shall suit myself in whatever I do. If I'm invited to his house and I want to go then I'll go.'

Will sat back, offended.

The rest of the evening seemed to be rather dreary and she asked Will to take her back early. She felt rather dispirited. She wasn't sure whether it was because Will had irritated her or what he'd said about Mark. Or perhaps it was the AZT.

For three days she didn't see anything of Mark. He was working at a distant hospital and his place was taken by the consultant, Mr Edwards. She found him a little remote and far more formal than Mark but a very competent man nevertheless.

Together they leaned over a man brought up from A and E, suffering from acute pains in the abdomen. She had introduced herself and tried to put the man at his ease. Then she'd taken a quick medical history. Pain in the abdomen, getting progressively worse. He'd been sick, his tongue was coated and his breath smelled. Temperature was up. When she examined the abdomen she found pronounced tenderness at the place known as McBurney's point.

'What do you find, Dr Grey?' the consultant asked.

She ran a quick check in her mind—was there anything she'd overlooked? 'Appendicitis. I think it should come out promptly to avoid the danger of peritonitis.'

'I agree. Would you like to do it at once?'

'On my own?'

He looked at her calmly. 'I take it you have done several under supervision?' She had. 'Then organise yourself a theatre and an anaesthetist. It's a very minor operation. I will, of course, be available should anything go wrong.'

Her anaesthetist was Mary-Lou Day. The two dressed in greens, scrubbed up together then entered the theatre. There was no problem to the operation. Rosalind made the incision, cut through the fat and muscles down to the inflamed sac, tied it off and cut it out, then neatly stitched it. It didn't take long and it wasn't hard, but when she'd finished she was conscious she'd done a good job.

'Exciting, isn't it, the first operation you do completely on your own?' Mary-Lou asked as they threw their greens into the laundry sack. 'Are you thinking of becoming a surgeon?'

'I've considered it,' Rosalind said cautiously.

'You should. We need more female surgeons. And you've got a talent for it, I can tell. Come and have a coffee in the canteen with me.' It was more an instruction than a request, and Rosalind went.

'Are you learning plenty, working hard, taking advice from your seniors?' Mary-Lou asked cheerfully as they sat in the largely deserted canteen.

'Trying to,' Rosalind said guardedly. She wasn't sure where this conversation was leading.

'Then I've got some advice for you. Don't go out with

older men. They're dangerous.' This came with an even
bigger grin than before.

'Why are they dangerous?'

Mary-Lou waved a biscuit expansively. 'I don't know.
Because they're older, I guess.'

'Do I take it that you've been prompted to warn me?'

'That's a good guess. I knew you were shrewd.'

'You've been prompted by your SHO, Will Roberts?'

'I cannot divulge a confidence, medical or otherwise.
Us doctors have got to stick together. Why, is Will your
boyfriend?'

Rosalind smiled icily. 'He was until thirty seconds
ago.'

'Hope it was nothing I said,' Mary-Lou murmured,
and Rosalind had to laugh.

'Tell me, why did you deliberately make Will look
bad? You could have been a lot more tactful.'

'I could. I'd have done a favour for Will, he's a good
SHO, but the big squirt wouldn't rely on my good sense
and good nature—he tried to blackmail me. Blackmail
me! Said he was sure I didn't want gossip about me and
Mark Harrison. I take it we are talking about Mark?'

Rosalind was feeling bewildered. 'He's just a friend,'
she said. 'Nothing to me, really.'

'Really?' Mary-Lou asked laconically. 'Well, your
newly ex-boyfriend, Will, will make a good anaesthetist
in time. I mean that. But it's a good thing that his patients will be mostly unconscious. Though he could bore
them unconscious. That'd be a new kind of anaesthetic.
Tell me, kid, didn't he ever bore you?'

'He knows a lot of medicine,' Rosalind said weakly.
But the realisation was dawning. Will *had* bored her.

'Lot of medicine, my ass,' Mary-Lou said inelegantly.

'I'll quote from a friend of yours. Medicine is about people, not diseases.' She paused. 'I was meant to scare you off by telling you about my affair with Mark so I will.'

'Let me get you another coffee,' Rosalind said hastily, and rose to rush to the counter. This conversation was moving too fast—she needed to think a minute. Should she tell Mary-Lou that she wasn't interested in gossip? But she really did want to hear about Mark. Wasn't it being unfaithful to talk behind his back? But she liked Mary-Lou, liked her earthy charm and honesty.

'Decided to listen to me?' Mary-Lou asked with a grin when she returned with two coffees. 'Good. Perhaps I can help two people I like.'

'I had a brief fling with young Mark. He was witty, charming, kind, considerate, always good company. And he made it clear from the start that this was not going to be the love affair of the century. We were both lonely, and we were good for each other.'

'Lonely?' Rosalind asked, perplexed. 'He's very popular. He's got lots of friends, everybody likes him.'

'Lonely,' Mary-Lou said firmly. 'We were good for each other and nobody got hurt. He's a lovely man, Rosalind. Don't you think so?'

'I suppose so,' Rosalind muttered.

'What you won't know is that he's also a wonderful lover.'

This seemed to be carrying frankness too far. 'How can you say such a thing?' Rosalind asked, blushing slightly.

'I can say it because it's true. For another, I know that, of all the women in this hospital, you won't repeat this conversation.' She drained her cup. 'Do I have to

go back to the States to get a good cup of coffee? Ugh!'
She stood to leave.

'I've got a question,' Rosalind said hastily. 'What did
you mean when you said perhaps you could help us?'

Mary-Lou appeared to consider. 'I guess I don't
know,' she said. 'Thanks for the coffee.'

Rosalind went back to the ward.

In the afternoon there was more paperwork—drug
requisitions to fill in, reports to write. Rosalind now
found she could do it much more quickly and just as
efficiently.

When she had an odd minute she thought about her
conversation with Mary-Lou. Mark Harrison lonely? She
was perplexed. Every time she learned something new
about Mark Harrison's character it added another di-
mension, revealed a depth she hadn't suspected. He was
a fascinating man.

It happened suddenly. She'd always been able to bury
herself in her work and could concentrate on her studies
until they drove out physical or mental pain. Then there
was a shock as she reappeared into the real world.

She was looking through a report from the lab on a
blood sample. A blood sample! The memory of her
needlestick injury flashed back. She'd have to give a
blood sample soon to see if she was HIV positive.

She went to pour herself a coffee, more for something
to do than any real need for the drink. Then she flipped
open a doctor's magazine. There was a table of deaths
through AIDS in the past ten years. She could be one of
those statistics soon. Terror seized her. All she could do
was wait for it to pass.

One thing she had made up her mind about was Will.
They'd had some reasonable times together but since

she'd started as a houseman she'd seen little of him, and on reflection she didn't want to see more. Besides, he'd talked about her—tried to manipulate her.

He phoned the next day, asking her to go out for dinner again. She pleaded pressure of work and suggested a quick lunch in a local pub.

He was late so she ordered a ploughman's for him. When he entered she turned her head as he bent to kiss her. She didn't like blatant expressions of affection in public. Besides, he was too possessive.

'Sorry I'm late,' he started, 'but we had an interesting case in and I wanted to discuss it afterwards with the specialist registrar. The patient was a gall bladder, very fat and with…'

Rosalind wondered how much the specialist registrar had wanted to discuss the case. Why had she never noticed how self-absorbed he was, how incapable of recognising what other people were thinking? Not like—

She broke into his monologue. 'Will, I don't think we should see each other any more.' She'd said it because she'd been irritated, and now she wondered if she hadn't been a bit brutal.

'But…but…' he spluttered. He was speechless.

She tried to make amends. 'Look, Will, you're busy, I'm busy. We've had some good times but that was then. We're not getting anywhere so we may as well—'

'I thought we were getting somewhere,' he interrupted angrily. 'I know you've got some strange ideas but— This is Harrison's fault, isn't it?' His voice rose. 'He's turned your head. I told you he was a womaniser. You don't know what you're doing.'

Some part of Rosalind smiled cynically. Poor Will, he

couldn't have said a worse thing. But she didn't lose her temper.

'It is not Dr Harrison's fault, he hasn't turned my head and I do know what I am doing. I don't want anything to do with a man who discusses me with his colleagues.'

'Discusses you! Who…? What…?'

'Mary-Lou did what you asked her. She warned me about Mark. But it was obvious that she'd been prompted. I won't be manipulated, Will.'

'I'll go.' He rose, looking angrier than she'd ever seen him. Then he leaned forward so his face was only inches from hers. She didn't move back—there was no way Will would ever intimidate her.

'You'll get nowhere with that man,' he spat. 'He'll use you like he used the others. He's married, you know. I'll bet he hasn't told you that. He left his wife behind in London. A chap I met on the course told me—said he'd trained with them both and they were real love-birds. Goodbye!' Will strode off.

Rosalind was shaken, not by Will's ineffectual anger but by the fact that Mark was married. She should have known—men like Mark got married young. Will was certainly telling the truth. He didn't have enough imagination to make up something like that.

She couldn't work out why she was so upset. Mark Harrison was a friend, that was all.

CHAPTER SEVEN

'IT's been a while,' Mark said after the ward round three days later. 'Come to tea tonight. I bought some smoked salmon this morning. We'll have smoked salmon sandwiches.'

He always made Rosalind feel happy. On the ward, where there was so often turmoil, grief and indeed death, his calmness and cheerfulness always made a welcome respite.

'Salmon sandwiches?' she asked. 'Very aristocratic. Am I going to get thin brown bread with the crusts cut off, rolled up in a nice genteel manner?'

He looked at her in horror. 'Certainly not. If it doesn't take two hands to hold it's not a sandwich. Besides, crusts make my hair curl.' He pulled at the blond strands.

She laughed, then recollected that Will had said Mark was married. If he saw the doubt or anger on her face he said nothing. She caught herself. She had always prided herself on her self-possession. She wasn't going to question him here.

'All right,' she said. 'What time shall I come?'

They arranged for just after six but, in fact, it was nearly seven by the time she lifted the ornate knocker. It had been the usual problem, too many tasks and not enough hands. You couldn't walk away from urgent work.

'I've got something to ask you, Mark, and I want an honest answer,' she started the moment she got inside.

Over the past two hours the question had been churning inside her, making her angrier and angrier. She knew she sounded harsh and disagreeable.

He held up his hands in defence. 'You can ask me anything. But I'll bet you've had nothing to eat since breakfast. I've watched you—your blood sugar's at rock bottom. You're irritable, liable to take wrong decisions, say things you don't mean. So eat then ask questions.'

Logic told her he was right, though she still felt angry. She silently sat at the table and ate the sandwiches he had provided. As before, they were wonderful, but made with salmon instead of ham. And as she ate she felt her anger dissolving.

'I needed that,' she said when she had finished the first one. 'But you knew it, didn't you?'

'Even doctors are susceptible to fatigue,' he said. 'Sometimes they forget.'

She went on, 'And the sandwich was really nice. I like smoked salmon.'

'Cookery is like medicine. To get ahead you have to specialise. I am now a consultant sandwich-maker.'

He was right, she did feel better. But her anger returned. If he was married he should have told her. She didn't ask herself why she had the right to know, she just knew she did.

As before, they took their second cups of tea to sit relaxed, she on the couch and he against the wall.

'Now ask your question,' he said. 'If it's a medical one I'll do the best I can to answer it honestly. You're obviously upset about something.'

He thought she was worried about the risk of HIV infection. She had managed to push that to the back of her mind, if only for a while.

'Are you married?' she asked bluntly. 'Let me say in advance that I'm not very happy with people whose marriages don't "work out". My mother felt things weren't working out and left my father with three daughters to bring up. I'm not keen on divorce either. And, for once, don't joke about things.'

His usual cheerful expression had gone. Instead, there was a wariness, perhaps even a sadness. He didn't answer her, and the silence dragged on unendurably. She thought about what she'd just said and realised she'd been far, far too pushy. 'I'm sorry,' she mumbled. 'It's not my business and I—'

'Wait a minute,' he said. 'I'll answer your question. Perhaps I should have told you before.'

He rose swiftly to his feet and ran upstairs. When he returned he gave her a picture, face down, and settled again in his old position.

She glanced from him to the picture in her lap. 'When I look at this picture, will it change things between us?'

'Possibly. I like to think not.' His voice was calm.

She turned the picture over. It was the face of a young girl—or woman, really, in her early twenties. She had raven hair, worn long, and brown eyes. Rosalind could see she was beautiful but it wasn't the beauty that was so entrancing. The girl was smiling, and she looked out of the picture at a future that was inexpressibly bright. Perhaps she was in love. Whatever it was, no one could fail to react to the hope in those eyes. Rosalind knew she'd like the girl.

She stared at the picture. Then she asked Mark, 'Who is it?'

'That was Frances, my wife. She died of AIDS six years ago.' Rosalind's body jerked forward, her fingers convulsing where they held the picture. He reached to try to take it from her but she didn't want to let it go. He came to sit next to her and put his arm round her, comforting her.

'I'm sorry, Rosalind, that was unforgivable. I just didn't think!'

She managed to speak. 'It doesn't matter, it doesn't matter. Mark, I was so rude to you and I...I didn't know. I—'

'That doesn't matter either,' he interrupted. 'I would have told you in time. Most people I don't tell—you I would have.'

She liked it there with his arm around her. When he made to move away she caught his arm and pulled it back around her. It was comforting.

'Is it because of her that...that you take such care of me?'

'No. Well, perhaps a little. I'm concerned for you— well, because I am. I'd be equally concerned if you'd been exposed to say, serum hepatitis.'

'Do I get a choice?' she managed to joke in a small voice.

'I'm afraid not.' There was silence for a moment.

She asked, 'Will you tell me about it? I'd like to know, but don't talk if it's painful.'

He shook his head. 'It's better to talk when you can. It's not something you can bottle up.'

She turned to rest her head against his chest, and could feel the powerful beat of his heart. 'Tell me, then.'

His voice seemed calm, but she thought she could detect a throb of emotion underneath. 'Frances was two years younger than me, training to be a doctor in the same hospital in London. We married when she qualified and was starting her housemanship. Like you. I was an SHO.'

'Is that why you're so kind to Eric? Because he's just got married?'

He shrugged. 'Perhaps. Though Frances and I didn't have many problems. Anyway, we didn't see too much of each other, but we were wonderfully happy. We got a tiny residency flat and the flat and the hospital were our lives. We hardly moved out. When she finished her housemanship she went to Africa for six months. It was something she'd promised herself she would do. An old friend was working out there who'd helped her. I didn't want her to go, and I couldn't go myself, but, of course, I didn't stand in her way.'

'Anyway...who can say how it happened? AIDS was pandemic there—they called it Slim. She took all possible precautions, but when she came back she was infected.'

'It took her three years to die. I wanted to leave the hospital so we could be together, but she said I had to do something more for her—carry on working. So I did, and eventually she died. It took a lot of getting over. I couldn't stay on the same hospital so when the chance came I applied for the job of Specialist Registrar and came up here. And I tried to lose myself in work.'

'I know,' she said. 'Alex told me.'

'I suppose I was overdoing it. Then the chance came to go to Malapa island. I went, and I think I sorted myself out there. Perhaps even you helped, young Grey. Mourning is natural and so is grief, but it mustn't take over your life. Frances told me that she was dying but that I must live. So, partly in memory of her, I do.'

By this time Rosalind couldn't contain herself. Tears

were running down her face. 'I don't know if I'm crying for myself or for you,' she sobbed. 'No one makes me cry, but you have.'

He stroked her back, a steady soothing movement that comforted her. 'It doesn't matter. Cry if you wish.'

She slid down so her head was in his lap. He leaned over and pulled up her legs. Her eyes closed and she fell asleep—it had been hard on the ward.

After half an hour she woke. 'You must have cramp,' she said. 'You haven't moved.'

'I kept the blood moving by tensing and relaxing the muscles but not moving my leg.'

'Romantic as ever. I can see why all the girls fall for you.' She sat up and kissed him. It seemed the obvious thing to do.

It was a simple kiss. She wrapped her arms round his neck, kissed each cheek and then his lips. At first his arms stayed by his sides, but then, with infinite delicacy, he held her and pulled her to him.

She didn't know how it happened. She had started to kiss a man she liked and admired, who was helping her. But when her lips touched his her safe, organised world lurched and she knew it would never be the same again. She'd never felt this way before. She didn't just like Mark. She loved him.

Somehow Mark realised what she was feeling. His grasp tightened as she murmured his name. He kissed her like a lover, as if nothing were forbidden between them. His hand caressed her neck and slid down to the warmth between her shoulder and her shirt. She moaned, pushing herself against him. Her mouth opened under the insistence of his lips.

His phone rang.

Neither of them moved for a moment, as still as if carved from granite. The phone still rang.

Sadly he eased her away from him. 'The expression is saved by the bell,' he said. 'I'm on call.'

She didn't move as he walked to the phone. Too much had happened too quickly. How could he act as if things were the same as five minutes ago? Didn't he know how she felt? Didn't he feel the same?

He was talking to the sister on the ward. 'Yes, I know about Mr Applegate... Wife and daughter there? Yes, I know the SHO will have tried... Well, if they're asking especially for me then I'll come over... Try not to get their hopes up.'

He came and sat on the couch again, but at the far end—not by her.

'You're going to the ward,' she said reproachfully.

'I don't have to, but I will. It's Ron Applegate.'

'I saw him this afternoon, Poor man, he hasn't got long.' The doctor in her was warring with the girl and lover. 'Why do you have to go? You know there's nothing you can do for Ron.'

'Nothing for Ron, but I might be of some comfort to his wife and daughter.'

'You must go, then.'

They looked at each other steadily. 'What about us?' she asked. It was a question to which she didn't know the answer.

'Yes, what about us? It was getting out of control, Rosalind. Things were going too far.'

'I'm a big girl now, Mark. I make decisions. I was happy to go along with what happened. And don't you dare say you're sorry!'

He shook his head, more in bafflement than in denial.

'I'm not sorry, Rosalind. What you gave me, what you showed me, was wonderful. But it was only kissing.'

'So far. We were going further.' She couldn't keep calm any longer. 'And I wanted to!' she shouted.

'I did, too. So it's up to me—because I'm older, wiser, senior, better-paid, bigger and more frightened. I've got to stop it. Now it's time for you to go.'

Perhaps she should go. She reached over and kissed him, this time quickly. 'I think you're marvellous,' she said.

Mark needed the five-minute walk between home and the ward to wrench his attention to what he now had to do. What had happened between him and Rosalind had disturbed him deeply. He had to have time to think, to sort out what he should do. But first he was a doctor. He had to deal with Ron Applegate.

Ron had been a big healthy man, working on one of the farms just outside town. He had loved his work and, like so many outdoor workers, he had smoked—heavily. He hadn't thought much about the pain in his chest—it might have been a muscle strain or the after-effects of a cold. But it had persisted.

His wife finally persuaded him to see his GP, and the GP sent him straight for an X-ray. The results were only too obvious. Ron almost certainly had lung cancer and was admitted to hospital for an immediate operation, a bronchoscopy. The surgeon inserted the thin, flexible tube into the lungs and sighed at what he saw. He cut off a tiny piece of tissue and sent it immediately to the lab.

The phone call came straight to the Theatre while Ron

was still unconscious and the surgeon still prepared to operate. 'I have a frozen section result for you.'

A nurse held the phone to the surgeon's ear. Only he could take the message. 'Thank you,' he said.

There would be no operation. The cancer was far too widely spread. It was inoperable.

To save him from pain Ron was now on massive doses of morphine, pumped into his arm. He lay unconscious in a curtained bed, his wife and daughter by his side. Mark had spoken to them several times. Now they wanted to speak to him again so he took them to the doctors' room.

'I'm afraid Ron's condition is very bad indeed,' he said. 'It's deteriorating from hour to hour. I'm afraid we can't hold out any hope.'

'That's why we wanted to see you,' Mrs Applegate whispered. 'You've been very good, Doctor. We thought we might ask you. If there's anything you can do—any operation, any chance, even if it's one in a million—we want you to try it. Can you do something for us, please? We've read in the papers…' Her voice trailed away.

He'd come across this before, the sheer desperation, the desire, to do something that might just possibly help. Sometimes he thought that films and television were to blame. He'd seen too many 'miracle cures' on screen. But he couldn't allow these two the luxury of hope.

'Everything that could possibly be done has been done,' he told them gently. 'Ron will die soon. You must let him die in peace. Now I'll take you back to his bedside. And I'll stay in here if you should want me.'

He knew it was pointless but if it helped Mrs Applegate and her daughter he was willing to do it.

Ron died two hours later. Mother and daughter accepted it and thanked Mark for what he had done. The daughter was petite, aged about eighteen. She reminded him just a touch of Rosalind.

Back at Gingerbread Hall Mark cleared away the cups and plates he and Rosalind had abandoned. He smoothed the couch where she'd sat, and wondered if he could smell the fresh scent of her hair on the leather. Then he made himself coffee and sat in his favourite place with his back to the wall. The couch was in front of him. It looked empty.

He thought about the family he'd just left. Ron, he knew, was thirty-seven, four years older than he himself. The daughter was about eighteen. Five years younger than Rosalind, they could easily have been sisters. He was ten years older than Rosalind. It was a complete generation.

He had to face it—he was too old for her. He was well qualified and he'd soon be a consultant. He had been married, had had affairs and at times he felt battered by life.

Rosalind was just starting her professional career, but in a sense she'd been in medical education all her life. She was wiser but less streetwise than other girls of the same age. Between them was a gap that was greater than ten chronological years.

But she was older than her years! She was brighter, more mature, more assured than the other little housemen he'd dealt with. And he was, he knew, in better shape than many men of his age and eminence. There was chronological age and real age. He always found time for exercise, and distanced himself from the narrow medical mind that so many of his colleagues seemed to acquire. And he and Rosalind blended so well!

Accept it, he told himself, you're attracted to her. Attracted to her far more than he had been to the other women he'd known recently. He'd had three affairs, pleasant and harming no one but essentially casual. He was still friendly with the three women. There was no question that what he felt for Rosalind was very different, far deeper than what he'd felt for them.

His feelings were not affected by his love for his dead wife, Frances. He'd managed to put that behind him. He knew that Frances, whom he would always love in some way, wouldn't have wanted him to remain single. He remembered something she'd said to him when they'd both known she was dying. She hadn't yet become semiconscious because of the morphine, prescribed to ease her pain.

'You're a man, Mark,' she had said. 'You have a man's feelings. You're to mourn me, but then you're to look for somebody else. Promise me you will.'

He had told her not to be foolish. He had been close, but had not yet come to the stage where he could have looked down at her wasted face and said to her that he knew there was absolutely no hope. Both had known she would die, but to have said so would have made it even more real.

She'd hurt him deliberately, knowing it would have the desired effect. 'Don't lie to a dying woman, Mark. Promise me you'll look for someone else!' So he had promised, for the first time shedding tears.

Frances had died and he had mourned her, thinking that never would he want to look at another woman.

He'd lost himself in work. But grief passed, and in time he'd met women to whom he was attracted.

He'd always started an affair by suggesting that the relationship was to be a fun one. He hadn't want to cheat anyone by promising more than he could deliver. But if anything did develop, he had thought to himself, then perhaps they could think again. Nothing ever had developed.

He had now found—he must own up to it—a woman he could love. No, a woman he *did* love. But she was ten years younger than him! The thought flashed across his mind of Ron Applegate and his daughter. There was too great a gulf between them. With the toughness he knew he had, he decided that Rosalind was not for him. What made it harder was that he knew she thought she loved him. She couldn't!

He'd suffered before, he could do it again. But he'd have to stay close to her. Because of Frances, he knew what agonies she was going through. The thought that she might be HIV positive would be with her constantly. She was resilient but she needed support. He had to help her. And if that was hard on him then it was too bad.

His coffee was cold. He went to a cupboard and took out a whisky bottle. Then he looked at it and put it back. He'd make more coffee. Too many men of his acquaintance had found that ultimately there were no answers to be found in solitary drinking. But he didn't sleep well that night.

'I think it was the salmon,' Mark said to Rosalind next morning when they had a moment together off the ward. 'It made us act like a couple of teenagers on our first date. It's because it's a fish. Caviar and oysters are both well-known aphrodisiacs. They cause you to act madly, wildly, without thought for the consequences.'

'They also cause you to enjoy yourself,' she pointed out.

'That's not the point! Are we agreed that smoked salmon sandwiches have a hitherto undocumented effect on men and women?'

She decided to go along with him. 'We are agreed. But there's undoubtedly the need for further research then we can write a paper for the *Journal of Endocrinology*.'

'Or even *Woman's Journal*,' he suggested.

'So all we need to agree on is what experiments are necessary.'

They looked at each other in silence. The jokes were still funny, but both of them remembered what had so nearly happened the night before.

'I told you not to say you're sorry,' she said accusingly, 'but you are—you're just wrapping it up.'

He shook his head. 'No. I'm just telling you that the next sandwich you get will be made with meat paste. No more smoked salmon. Meat paste is safe.'

She felt slightly rebellious. 'What happens if I say I really like smoked salmon?'

He tapped her on the shoulder. 'You're a trouble-maker, young Grey. Kindly remember that you're a lowly houseman and I am an important registrar. The older doctor knows best. No more smoked salmon.'

That's a funny word for it, she thought to herself. She knew exactly what he meant. They were to be friends, not lovers. How did she feel about that? She wasn't sure. But something inside her was very disappointed.

* * *

It wasn't Mark beside her in the operating theatre. Even when he was gowned and masked in his greens he somehow managed to convey a sense of friendliness. Today she was by the side of the consultant, and Mr Edwards was a more remote figure than Mark. They were repairing a hiatus hernia together, where some of the stomach had displaced through the opening in the diaphragm into the chest.

To Rosalind's surprise, Mr Edwards had invited her to make the initial incision, and to retract skin and muscle. Eventually she turned, expecting Mr Edwards to take over.

'You have observed this procedure before, Dr Grey?' he asked.

'Several times,' she answered.

'Very good. You may carry on and do it.'

'I'm to do it?' She was surprised.

There was no indication of emotion from the impassive eyes above the green mask. 'If you do not feel capable then, of course, I will.'

'I'd like to carry on.'

He took no further part in the operation but she noticed he watched everything she did. Eventually she finished and closed. She knew that her suturing was better than normal—she seemed to have the natural dexterity for it.

'Very good, Doctor,' Mr Edwards said abruptly. 'I think our work here is now finished.'

She followed him as he entered the corridor. Like him, she pulled off her cap and slipped down her mask.

'After your time with us you're doing six months' medical?' he asked.

'Yes, sir. The normal houseman's stay.'

'Looking forward to it?'

She wondered if there was more to the question than was obvious. 'There's a lot I have to learn, but I do enjoy surgery.'

'Quite so. Have you thought about your future career? Are you going to be a GP?'

On this point she was certain. 'No. I want to be a hospital doctor.'

'Have you considered surgery?'

Being asked this by the consultant surgeon was really something, but she tried to keep calm as she answered. 'I know it's difficult, a popular choice and there aren't many women doing it. But, yes, I'd like ultimately to concentrate on surgery.'

Perhaps it was the right answer. He continued, 'Yes, it is difficult, if only because a large number of people don't realise that most of a surgeon's work is done before he puts on greens and enters the theatre. But—and I say no more than this, Dr Grey—I think you might have the necessary physical skills for the job. Please don't read more into my remark than I intend.'

This was it. 'Would you have me on your firm in a year or so?'

He wasn't going to commit himself so far in advance. He said, 'If and when you apply I think I'd be inclined to look favourably on your application. Other things being equal, of course.'

For the cautious Mr Edwards that was equal to an engraved invitation. She could hardly contain her jubilation. 'Thank you, sir,' she said.

The elated feeling was still with her as she walked round the ward that afternoon. It must have been obvious.

'You've got a silly grin,' Mark said, suddenly appearing like a genie from a bottle. 'Don't tell me, you've won the lottery. I demand ten per cent.'

'Nearly as good as the lottery,' she said. There was no one she'd rather share this news with than Mark. 'I've just done a hiatus hernia for Mr Edwards. He said I might have the skills to be a surgeon.'

'He said that?'

'Well, not straight out. Lots of ifs and buts. But he said it might be possible and there could be a place for me on his firm.'

'Fantastic! For him that's better than a contract.' After a quick, wary look around, he pulled her behind a curtained bed and kissed her. 'Mustn't excite the patients,' he whispered. 'Bad for their blood pressure.'

Just as quickly he led her from behind the bed. 'We'll walk down the ward like a couple of colleagues discussing difficult medical problems. Which, in a sense, we are.'

She blinked. Had he kissed her?

He went on, 'I've not said it yet, young Grey, but I agree with him. I'm being a bit unprofessional now. We get housemen coming through here and most of them learn something. They're going to be GP's or paediatricians or whatever. They need to work on a surgical ward to learn but that is all. Neither Alison nor Eric will ever be surgeons, though they'll both be good doctors. But you are the best houseman that we've had in the past three years.'

'I want to be a surgeon, Mark, I really do!' For a moment she was carried away. It all seemed so possible!

Then he saw the enthusiasm in her face drain away. She'd remembered. 'If I haven't got the HIV virus,' she said. There was no way she could carry out invasive surgery if she were infected.

Mark's face froze, too. 'At present you haven't,' he said. 'You're feeling no ill-effects and there's no way you could affect your patients. Remember that. Now, don't feel sorry for yourself—go and get on with your work. Some people here *know* they're going to die.'

'Sorry, Mark,' she said briefly. 'It won't happen again. I'll go and finish those reports you wanted.'

He watched her as she walked away. Did I say that to her? he asked himself. *Did I say that to her?* Did I speak so harshly to a girl who might have the HIV virus? A girl I...could...love?

Some calmer part of his mind answered, Yes, that's what you said to her. And if it were necessary you would say it again.

Rosalind knew they were being gossiped about and she didn't really mind. It was part of hospital life. She knew that both her sisters and their husbands had heard the gossip and wanted to know what was happening. There was no need to lie to them so she said that Mark was just a very good friend.

She had told Mark that he was an extra brother-in-law.

'I know both of the other two,' he said. 'I think that's a compliment.'

'It's meant as one,' she told him. 'I need somebody I can turn to.'

'Somebody safe,' he said.

But Lisa wasn't very impressed with her story. 'Sisters are here to help,' she said to Rosalind one day. 'I've

known you since you were one day old. You're keeping
something from us.'

Rosalind was shocked at Lisa's perception, but she
still shook her head. 'I'd tell you if there was anything
to tell. But there isn't.'

'If my baby is a girl I might call her Rosalind. Does
that mean she'll keep secrets, like you?'

'She'll have to be clever to keep anything from her
mother. No, Lisa, gossip is a hospital cottage industry.
There's nothing in it.'

She *was* attracted to Mark—no, she loved him. But
she thought he valued her friendship and had decided he
wasn't going to spoil that for the sake of quick sexual
gratification. What she felt about that she still wasn't
quite sure.

At intervals she had the blood tests, done by Mark.
There was little chance of anything showing yet, but
they had to go through the procedure. Ultimately there
would either be a positive reaction or so much time
would have elapsed that they could safely decide she
was free of infection. Until that time she had to wait.

Sometimes, at night or after she'd been working too
hard, the horror of the situation would hit her. It was
waiting for total freedom—or a death sentence. There
was nothing in between. If she was with Mark she would
pull him onto the couch, put her arms round him and
push her head into his chest, taking comfort from his
sheer closeness.

She had no social life outside the hospital, but she
was learning. Work on the ward was different from when
she had been a student. Then cases had been presented,
they had been discussed and an answer given by the
lecturer or doctor in charge. But on the ward the sheer

messiness of life intruded. Dealing with relatives was often as big a problem as the clinical case itself. But she enjoyed it.

She had to learn to be more outgoing. In the past she had hidden behind a blank face and a quick brain. Mark told her that in medicine that wasn't good enough.

'I know you're loveable really, Rosalind, but patients and relatives don't know that. You've got to relax, smile a bit—pretend, if you like. Remember, people need comfort as well as medicine. If you can reassure them they'll get better quicker.'

It was a good message. And when she tried to put it into practice she found that it made her job easier.

Mark was away in London for the day when the case came in. It had been a hot, sticky day and she was looking forward to getting back to her room to change and shower. Her patients were irritable in the heat and humidity.

'Got one that needs admitting,' the voice from A and E said tersely. 'It's an RTA. Broken legs, trauma to head and, we think, internal injuries.'

'I'm on my way down,' she said.

She'd now often been to the A and E department, but it still made her think of things that were better forgotten. This time it was worse. Harry Dempsey, the male nurse who had been with her when she was attacked, was waiting. He took her into the doctors' room.

'I recognised the woman,' he said. 'Louie Bell. The police have brought her in before—collapsing in the streets, that sort of thing. She's an addict, Rosalind, got full-blown AIDS. Are you OK?'

'There's no reason anyone else should deal with her,' Rosalind said.

She was led into the curtained cubicle. There was a thin figure on the trolley and a drip had been set up. On the wall behind were illuminated X-rays. Mike, the A and E consultant, was leaning over, palpating the woman's abdomen. When he saw Rosalind he nodded at the X-rays on the wall.

'I've sent for the orthorpaedics man to look at the legs, but I'm more worried about this abdomen. Her pressure's down and there are no stomach sounds.'

She looked at the X-rays first. The legs weren't broken, they were shattered. It would take hours of work to reconstruct them. Then she moved over to feel the abdomen herself.

'Mr Edwards is on call,' she said. 'I'll go and bleep him.'

Louie was wheeled away. Rosalind joined her boss and the orthopaedic surgeon outside the theatre and the three of them quickly examined their patient and looked at the notes that had come with her. The orthopaedic surgeon raised his eyebrows at Mr Edwards. Mr Edwards looked at Rosalind. 'What d'you think, Rosalind?'

Flatly, Rosalind said, 'A young woman, badly nourished and very liable to infection. We know she has AIDS. Bones are badly damaged but most important are the internal injuries. She may well have a ruptured spleen or liver. Certainly she's losing blood internally at a tremendous rate.'

'So is there any point to this operation?'

'I doubt it. She'll probably die. But she'll certainly die if we don't operate. So we go ahead.'

'A lucid and accurate summing-up,' Mr Edwards said.

Louie was taken to be prepped for Theatre and Rosalind joined the other two, scrubbing up. A disturbed-looking Mary-Lou Day looked round the door.

'Don't tell me,' Mr Edwards said. 'You don't advise this operation. The patient is far too weak. I agree. But there's nothing we can do. We've resuscitated as best we can. We've pumped her full of blood. We operate now or we just don't bother.'

'So long as you know how I feel,' said Mary-Lou.

This time Mr Edwards did most of the work himself, Rosalind merely assisting. Both liver and spleen were ruptured. Mr Edwards managed to repair the liver and excised the spleen. The orthopaedic surgeon decided not to attempt anything too ambitious. He could return if and when the patient got stronger. The two surgeons closed. Louie Bell was sent down to an intensive care bed.

Two hours later she died.

Mr Edwards and Rosalind looked at the still figure on the bed as a nurse set about dismantling equipment.

'Pity, really,' Mr Edwards said. 'Quite a young woman. I wonder how she contracted AIDS? I suppose it's always a danger with addicts. A healthy woman would have stood quite a good chance. Well, we did all we could.' He turned to leave.

Rosalind remained. There were things to do, relatives to be contacted—if there were any—the paperwork, always necessary after a death. She looked down at all that was left of Louie Bell. Would that be her in a year or two? Was this the inevitable end of HIV?

CHAPTER EIGHT

ROSALIND managed to get off at six. Outside it was more humid than ever. Her light cotton dress clung to her and her underwear felt like damp rags. The sky was a dark, dirty yellow colour. She didn't go back to her room. She was restless.

By now she should be accustomed to death, but the sight of Louie Bell's ravaged body had upset her. She knew that, whatever happened, she wouldn't turn to illegal drugs for comfort. Still, her death could be as inevitable as Louie's.

The sweat ran down her spine and between her breasts. Perhaps she should visit one of her sisters—but she didn't feel like it. She walked aimlessly around the hospital grounds, passing bits seldom visited or even seen. She saw a sign, showing the way to the mortuary. She winced, and walked on a little faster.

Perhaps it was inevitable that in time she should pass Mark's house. There was a light in the window of Gingerbread Hall, and she frowned. He had said he'd be back the next day so he must have returned early. For a moment she stood, irresolute, looking at the light sparkling through the varicoloured glass. Then she turned and walked purposefully towards the nearest hospital gate.

There was a small shopping precinct nearby, which stayed open late because of the trade from the hospital. She went to an upmarket delicatessen and bought a white wine she remembered Mark talking about. It was expensive. Then she walked back to Gingerbread Hall, getting stickier every minute.

When she knocked there was an unusually long wait. It gave her time to consider what she was doing here—she didn't really know. Then Mark opened the door, clad merely in a towel around his waist and one in his hand. His hair was wet, and tiny rivulets of water ran down his shoulders and over his chest. 'Rosalind?' he said, surprised. 'Come in.'

She stood just inside the door and said the first thing that came into her head. 'I thought you weren't coming back till tomorrow.'

'I came back early,' he said calmly. 'We finished sooner than we thought.'

'Why are you showering? Are you going out? Am I in the way?' She was gabbling, she knew.

He smiled. 'You'll never be in the way. I'm not going out and I've just showered because I was sticky after the journey.'

'I'm sticky, too,' she said. 'Everybody's sticky. I think there's going to be a storm.' She offered him the bag in her hand. 'I bought you some wine.'

He looked at the wine and pursed his lips in approval. 'We mustn't drink that while it's warm. I'll put it back in the fridge to re-chill. Are you all right, Rosalind?'

It came out in a rush, the words tumbling over each other. 'We had a patient this afternoon from A and E, an RTA. I operated with Mr Edwards this afternoon. And she died. She was badly injured but I think she really died because she had AIDS.'

'And you saw yourself there? Thought it could happen to you?'

'Yes. And I was frightened.'

He opened his arms to her and she hugged him, pushing herself against him. His arms were cool around her and his body was damp, faintly scented with the French Fern soap she knew he liked. Fretfully she said, 'You're all nice-feeling and I'm sticky and horrid.'

With a finger he traced her hairline. She knew he could feel the beads of sweat there. 'Yes, you are sticky,' he said mildly. 'Why don't you go and get a shower yourself? I'll even lend you a dressing-gown.'

'But—'

He turned her and eased her towards the stairs. 'You'll feel much better afterwards. You know where the bathroom is. Leave the door ajar a minute and I'll throw in the gown. And I'll put this in to chill.'

Events seemed to have taken her over. And the prospect of a shower was wonderful. 'All right,' she said.

First she washed herself with the warm jet, then slowly turned the control to tepid so her body cooled. He'd passed in fresh towels as well as the dressing-gown. She dried herself then slipped into the gown. It was silk. It was cool and caressed her skin.

She admired herself in the bathroom mirror. The gown came down to her feet—white with blue dragons writhing around it. It looked as lovely as it felt—but the overall effect was spoiled by her hair. She went downstairs.

'Is this yours?' she asked. 'I do like it.'

'Then have it. I bought it in San Francisco Chinatown and I've never worn it. I'd like it to have some use.'

'I couldn't possibly....'

'It doesn't fit me. It's either you or Oxfam.'

It was so comfortable, so tempting. She knew she couldn't offer him money but... 'I'll take it if you'll let me buy you something. A shirt or tie or whatever you like.'

He looked alarmed. 'No clothes, please. If you bought me a tie I'd have to wear it. And I might not like it. Women have no taste in men's ties.'

This was fighting talk. 'Judging by that brown thing round your neck last week, men have no taste either. And look at you. I hope you're not going on the ward like that.'

He'd changed while she'd been in the bathroom. He was wearing white shorts and a loose top. He looked cool. 'Clothes to suit the moment,' he said placidly. 'I really don't want anything, but if you feel uneasy then I'd like another bottle of that excellent wine you bought. Speaking of which…' He fetched two full glasses from the kitchen. 'I had to try it. Your taste is really good.'

'You told me about it,' she pointed out.

'Then my taste is really good.' He sipped. 'That is nectar, young Grey. Now, sit on the couch and I'll sit behind you.'

She saw he had a hairbrush in his hand, and he drew it gently through her wet hair. She'd always loved having her hair brushed. It brought back memories of bath nights, of her sisters or her father, doing just this.

'That's nice,' she sighed. 'You know just how to do it so it's calming and soothing. Where did you learn to…?' Her question went unfinished. She'd suddenly guessed the answer.

He noticed the break in her speech. 'I used to brush Frances's hair,' he said serenely. 'It pleased her and it pleased me. Rosalind, I told you about her because I wanted you to know. You mustn't be afraid to mention her—it doesn't hurt. Some part of her is part of me now.'

Without slowing the hypnotic brushing of her hair, he reached forward and grasped her wrist to feel for her pulse. 'You're less stressed now,' he said, 'Things should be getting easier.'

Suddenly the room was lit by a flash of incredible white light, bleaching everything of colour. Then it was dark again, and she closed her eyes in shock.

'Lightning,' he said, and as he spoke there was the deafening crash of thunder outside. She started. Storms didn't frighten her but this one seemed very close. 'A storm is just what we need,' he went on, and rose to turn off the lights.

It was now night. They heard the hiss and rattle of rain on the roof. They sat there in the lightning-pierced darkness, and as the turmoil of the elements raged outside she gradually grew calmer. It was good to sit here with him.

The lightning subsided and the cracks of thunder became less earth-shaking as the storm moved away. There was now only the rain, still noisy, and the coolness of a breeze from a half-open window. She felt so much better.

'It's not a medical term I know,' she said, 'but I think I got the horrors. I feel silly now. I should know better.'

Imperturbable as ever, Mark said, 'You weren't being silly. Stress hits people in different ways. And I've never known anyone react to pressure as well as you are doing. But I know the pressure is there.'

He'd finished her hair now. It was dry. She turned to face him on the couch. As he reached over to refill her glass their fingers touched. That was all it took.

She took his hand. 'Put your glass down,' she said,

placing her own on the floor. He did. Then she took his other hand.

They sat facing each other on the couch, holding hands. It was dark, but the darkness was comforting. A lamp on the road outside shone through the windows by the door, casting a pattern of tiny coloured squares on the carpet. His head was only a vague shadow, but she could see flecks of light where his eyes were.

She was content to wait. After a while he pulled her to him and kissed her. It was the natural, the obvious thing to do. It was what she wanted.

His lips were cool and gentle. When she slipped her arms around him she felt the smoothness of his skin and ran her fingertips across his back to his neck. Slowly she reclined so that her back was on the couch and he leaning over her. He feathered kisses down the side of her face and in the corners of her eyes. His tongue flickered at the edge of her ear.

She moaned and, lifting her hand to the back of his head, pulled him down so his lips found her open, receptive mouth.

He was harder, more passionate now, as they responded to each other's growing passion.

After a while she pushed him back, loosened her gown and slipped it from her shoulders.

'Rosalind,' he muttered. 'I...'

She put her fingers on his lips. 'We're past talking now. I don't want to talk any more.' He kissed her again and eased her back to lie full length on the couch. Then his lips and tongue roved down her naked body, searching for and caressing the soft, exciting places—her neck, the insides of her arms and above all, the hard, burgeoning tips of her breasts.

The froth of silk left around her hips was pulled aside, and he groaned at the beauty of her.

'Take me to bed,' she gasped. 'Mark, take me to your bed.'

He kissed her one more time, slipped his arms under her neck and thighs and swept her up. Her weight seemed to make no impression on him as he carried her upstairs and laid her very gently on his bed.

His bed was large. She lay there languorously, the white cotton sheets cool beneath her now fevered body and her hands behind her head. She was his to take.

His dark form paused by the edge of the bed, as if he was thinking again. 'Come to me,' she called anxiously.

There was the faint sound of his clothes, sliding to the ground. Then he was leaning over her and kissing her again. This time he didn't stop after his tongue had teased her breasts to aching, hard-peaked excitement. His head trailed down her body as she pulled his hands to her, urging his fingers to grasp, to hold. She moaned aloud as his lips reached the final secret place and her body arched and writhed with abandon.

But soon she wanted more. She clutched him to her, muttering disjointed commands. He was to come to her. He kissed her lips again, his breath warm on her face. She was underneath him and opened herself to him, like a flower seeking rain. She sobbed in anticipation and they finally came together. There was a moment of apprehension, not pain, and then she was urging him gently onwards. This she had never done before, but she found it easy and natural. She caught him on her own rising tide of need, then cried aloud as they reached an awesome pinnacle of passion together.

He lay half on top of her, and she kissed his warm

brow. 'That was wonderful,' she murmured to him. 'You are so good to me.' Then her eyes slowly closed.

An hour later they woke together, and she caught him to her again. This time they were slower, more anxious to please each other, to explore what pleasures they could take and give. Eventually there was another climax, seeming to go on and on, like waves beating incessantly against a cliff.

'I love you, I love you, Mark, I love you,' she cried. Then it was over. 'I'm going to sleep now,' she told him. After a while she was aware of him pulling the sheet over their cooling bodies.

Rosalind slept well, better than she had in ages.

It was the scent of coffee that finally woke her, that and the half-conscious feeling that something wonderful had happened to her. Then the bedroom door opened and she was fully awake.

Mark was holding a breakfast tray for her, with a pot of coffee, toast and marmalade. But he was also fully dressed in shirt and trousers. She was disappointed.

'Breakfast in bed,' he said. 'I thought you should lie in.'

'I want breakfast with you.'

He put the tray on her lap, and went to fetch his own coffee. She wriggled to the side of the bed. 'Won't you get in with me?'

He leaned forward to kiss her on the forehead, then shook his head. 'No. Drink your coffee, then we'll talk.'

She looked at him suspiciously. 'I don't like the sound of that.'

He didn't answer, but pointed at the window. 'Look.

The sun is shining. Isn't there a quotation about tomorrow being another day?'

Of course, she knew where it came from. 'Last line of *Gone with the Wind*. Mark Harrison, I keep on finding out you're a closet romantic.'

'Cry every time I see it,' he confessed. 'Now, do as you're told and drink your coffee, like me.'

They drank in silence. The feeling that something wonderful was to happen to her was slowly evaporating. Mark looked either stern or ill at ease—she couldn't tell which.

Finally he put down his coffee-mug. The rap of it on the bedside cabinet startled her. 'It's early,' he began, 'so we get things decided. Rosalind, last night shouldn't have happened.'

The cry was dragged out of her. 'It should! Don't you…? Didn't I…didn't I make you happy?'

He was more disturbed than she'd ever seen him. He rose to pace up and down the room. 'Yes, you know you made me happy! How could you ask? It was a night I'll never forget. You were…you were…' He stopped, and leaned over her. Then, to her disappointment, he stood again.

He went on. 'I feel I took advantage of you. You're under strain, no one more so. You came to me for comfort, and I slept with you.'

'But I wanted you to!'

'That's not the point!' Frustrated, he stamped up and down the room again. 'I'm older than you and I'm a doctor. I should have known better.'

'You're not *my* doctor.' He was making her angry. 'Mark, why d'you think I knocked on your door last night, holding a bottle of wine? If last night was wrong then it was as much my fault as yours. But—' she knew her voice was getting shaky '—I'd rather think of it as something wonderful we did together.'

She saw him move towards her, then deliberately hold himself back. 'It *was* wonderful,' he said through gritted teeth, 'which is why it's got to stop. Rosalind, you know I...I've got a great regard for you. I hope we can always be friends. But that must be all.'

She was really angry now. 'Don't I have anything to say about this? Don't I have feelings? Last night I said I loved you, and I meant it!'

He paled with the shock but he was still determined. 'Rosalind, you've been in training since you were sixteen and you're now at the beginning of your career. You must learn there's more to life than studying medicine. We're pushed together here in the hospital—it's an artificial life. You need to live more.'

'Nothing pushed me to you. I just want to be close to you.'

It was her last plea, and for a moment she thought it would work. He stood, silent. Then he said, 'Rosalind, you must help me. I'm a family friend, we two are friends. That's all we can be. I'm ten years older than you. You're just attracted to me because, well, you're in stress.'

We're much, much more than just friends, she wanted to scream, but she knew it was useless. 'All right, we're friends,' she muttered. 'But, Mark, don't let me ever hear you say you're sorry about last night.'

'No.' he said. 'I'll never say that.'

It was time to be practical, though she wanted nothing so much as to lie down and cry. 'Mark, are there likely to be any—repercussions after last night?'

At first he didn't know what she meant. Then he realised. 'Oh, no. I was careful. I took precautions.'

'You'd better go while I get dressed,' she said.

Two hours later Rosalind was sitting in the doctors' room on the ward, writing up some notes. On the edge of her consciousness she heard one of the nurses ask, 'What are you doing here?' A male voice replied. It made her stomach churn, her hand shake and her mouth go dry. 'Couldn't keep away from you, Nurse Rollins.' It was Mark's voice.

He stood in the doorway. 'All well? Any problems?'

The strain of appearing normal, casual, was hard, but she did it. 'Nothing I can't cope with, Mark.'

He came in and reached over her to flip through a filing cabinet. 'I just wanted those case notes on Mr Simon.' He was so close. 'Ah, these are the ones.' He touched her briefly on the shoulder and was gone.

She waited till the door had closed, then clutched her shoulder where he'd touched her. It felt like it burned.

Rosalind needed simple, uncomplicated comfort. She wanted to be among people who liked her, loved her, who didn't have strange ideas about what was right. After tea that evening she walked round to Lisa's house. It would be nice to play with the children, then sit and relax, doing nothing much.

'Dad's coming home,' said Lisa with a smile when she opened the door to Rosalind's knock. 'We got a letter this afternoon, I was going to phone you later. He's coming home next week.'

'Show me!' Rosalind demanded.

They had all missed their father. After their mother left and was later killed, he had brought them up. They'd been a close-knit family—Rosalind often wondered if it was a coincidence that they'd all ended up at the same hospital. And when they'd all finally started on their careers their father had said it was time to leave them alone. He'd wandered off to South America—he'd always been fascinated by it.

Typically, after being captured by guerillas, he'd become their friend and had willingly stayed with them to help them. He was that kind of man. But now he was coming home!

The letter was shorter than usual. He said he had so much to tell them, but soon he could tell them in person. And there'd be a surprise as well.

'What kind of surprise do you think it'll be? Rosalind asked.

Lisa shrugged happily. 'Who can tell? Perhaps he's brought home a pet—an iguana or something.'

'Where's he going to stay?'

'All organised. I phoned Emily, and she's happy for him to come here. It's the obvious place. There's plenty of room and he can look around a bit, before deciding what he's going to do next.'

'It'll be lovely to have him back,' Rosalind agreed. Only now was she realising how much she had missed him. Only after coming across so many wrecked families, crumpling under the strain, did she realise how well he'd done with them.

Three young daughters would have been a handful for any man. But he'd loved them, cherished them, brought them up well. A thought passed through her mind. Was she as strong as him? Could she cope with personal tragedy as he had done? She decided she could.

*   *   *

A week later they took two cars to drive to the airport. Stephen couldn't get off, but Alex drove Lisa in one car and Emily drove Rosalind and Lisa's two stepchildren in the other. Holly and Jack would not be left behind. 'It's nice, getting a new grandfather,' said Jack. Holly said her teacher wanted him to tell them all about South America.

Of course, they arrived early. Rosalind took Jack and Holly to watch the planes taking off while her two sisters had a coffee. They all kept an eye on the arrivals board. The plane was on time, and the sign flashed to say that it had landed. They moved to the concourse to greet him.

There was the usual wait, then people started to trickle through.

'He's there, look, he's there,' Lisa said excitedly. 'Dad, we're here.'

So he was. He was a bit thinner than they remembered, very brown and pushing an overloaded trolley. He was talking to a tall woman next to him. Then he heard the call, saw them, smiled and waved.

Rosalind saw tears in the eyes of Lisa and Emily, and even felt a lump in her own throat. Must be getting soft, she thought crossly to herself.

But she herself cried when she hugged him. 'My little girl has grown,' he said, and she remembered the many times he'd called her his little girl. He hugged her first. Then there was Emily and Lisa, a handshake for Alex and a special word for Holly and Jack. It was so, *so* good to be part of a full family again.

Behind their happy group Rosalind caught sight of the woman who had been talking to their father. She was standing by the trolley, smiling gently. Rosalind thought she looked to be in her late forties. Cascading down her back was long black hair, attractively streaked with grey, caught in a silver band. There was an impression of serenity about her, and of shrewdness.

Rosalind's father turned, took the woman by the arm and pulled her into the group. 'I want you to meet someone,' he said. 'This is Dr Aileen Wright. Not a medical doctor like you, but a doctor of anthropology. I met her in the village where I was staying and we got to know each other well.'

There was a pause as the two older people looked at each other. 'We're going to get married,' John Grey said.

Rosalind looked at Emily who looked at Lisa. 'That's nice,' Rosalind said faintly. 'I've always wanted a mother.' She moved forward to kiss the woman who was to become her stepmother.

Rosalind liked Aileen. She travelled back with them while John went with Lisa and Alex. Alex had insisted that she stayed with them—he wouldn't hear of her going to stay in a hotel. In spite of being jet-lagged, Aileen took the trouble to talk to Holly and Jack. She obviously liked children. From her blouse she took a large silver brooch for Holly to try on. She said Grandad had bought Holly one himself, and it was packed in the cases.

'I'll bet you helped him buy it,' Rosalind chipped in.

'Only a little,' said Aileen. 'For a man he has surprising taste. Wasn't he good with your clothes and so on when you were growing up?'

Rosalind thought back. Yes, he *had* been good about clothes. 'I just hadn't realised it before,' she said.

'My special field is jewellery,' Aileen went on, 'so I did suggest things. But we always agreed.'

'Why didn't Grandad tell us you were coming?' Holly asked.

Aileen smiled. 'I'll bet Rosalind and Emily know.'

'He always loved surprises,' Emily said. 'Surprise present, surprise party, surprise holiday.'

'You're a nice surprise,' Jack said.

'Why, thank you. I won't say how surprised I am to find how nice you all are. It's what I expected.'

Both Emily and Rosalind found it easy to talk to Aileen. Her voice was slow and musical, and she somehow made people feel good to be with her.

'I'll guess you never expected to have a new mother,' Aileen said. 'Please don't resent me, but I feel I know you all already. We've spent a lot of time talking about you. I've always wanted a family and I hope I can share in John's.'

Yes, Rosalind liked her.

'We're having a dinner party next Saturday,' Emily said over the phone a few days later. 'This time at my house. I suppose it's Dad's engagement party. We've all managed to get time off work, and we calculate you can do the same.'

Rosalind thought about her timetable. 'I can come easily,' she said. 'I'd like us to welcome Aileen into the family.'

'Bit late for that. She's one of the family already. Anyway, would you like to bring somebody? I know you've lost that Will-thingy. What about bringing Mark Harrison? He's a family friend.'

'I'll certainly ask Mark,' Rosalind said, 'just so long as everybody knows that he's only a friend and a colleague.'

'Of course he is.' Rosalind could hear the laughter behind her sister's voice, and it irritated her.

It was a good party. With Holly and Jack sitting down, there were ten at the table. Aileen and John were now over their jet lag and, for Rosalind, listening to her father was like old times. He'd always been a good story teller. Holly and Jack now doted on him.

Bringing Mark here was a bit of a self-imposed test. If she could carry it off here then she knew she was safe. Her feelings were firmly under control. Mark had been delighted to be invited. 'Is Emily as good a cook as Lisa?' he asked. 'Because if she is I'll not eat for three days before.'

'It's a dinner party,' she told him. 'Good conversation but not enough food.'

He shook his head. 'I just do not believe that of any of your family.'

She introduced Mark very firmly as a friend.

'She means not a boyfriend,' Mark explained. 'We're different. Everybody else here seems to be in love.'

'How d'you feel about being just a friend, then?' John asked.

'Left out. Terrible, isn't it?'

Everyone laughed, but Rosalind noticed Aileen looking at Mark thoughtfully. Mark slipped into the family circle so very easily. In fact, he was already a family friend. And he didn't spend all his time with Alex and Stephen, talking about medicine. Like her father, he was a good story-teller. Now he had the entire table laughing as he explained how Rosalind had looked after him on Malapa Island.

'So there I was in a high fever and I opened my eyes.

I had this maid called Matilda, and she was looking down at me. It had to be Matilda because there was no other young female in the house. And I remember thinking, Poor Matilda's gone very pale. And why has she dyed her hair red? I must get her a tonic of some kind. And then a voice said, "I'm nearly a doctor..."'

She felt a great love welling up for her family—and sorrow that Mark wasn't a part of it. She had to admit it now. She loved him. She thought that in his own way he loved her too, but he was a man bound by his own principles. There was nothing she could do but suffer and keep a smiling face.

Only after dinner, when people were sitting, drinking coffee, in the living room, did she find chance to have a few words with Aileen on her own. She wanted to because she felt she hadn't yet had her chance to offer her own welcome.

'I wanted to say how pleased I am that you're marrying Dad,' she said. 'I don't think he could have done better.'

'That's lovely to hear,' Aileen said gently, 'especially from you. It's often the youngest daughter that is most resentful. But I've found myself a ready-made family and I don't think I could have done better. Lisa and Emily are happy in their marriages. And you say Mark is just a friend?'

'Just a friend,' Rosalind confirmed. 'I'm happy with my career—perhaps I'll never marry. Ask the rest of the family.'

'Never is a long time.'

Lisa came into the kitchen to fetch the coffee-pot. 'Tell Aileen I'm the solitary one,' Rosalind called out. 'Tell her how I'm happy on my own.'

'Aileen, we despair, we really do. We try to give her a good example—two happily married older sisters—and she ignores our advice.' Lisa walked off with the coffee.

'John said you were self-sufficient. But it's often the solitary people who fall the hardest.'

'Not me. I've got my career. I'm thinking about surgery, you know. That's why I'm so close to Mark. He's helping me.'

'Quite so,' Aileen said, with the serenity that was so much of her character.

Rosalind wondered if she'd convinced her. Her father was happy with her story. But this woman was something new.

CHAPTER NINE

IT HAD been a long time since Mark had enjoyed a friendly evening as much as he had with Rosalind and her family. The food was good, of course, but the togetherness was better. Now he knew what he had missed in his own younger days. This family was loving, supportive, but not intrusive. He'd love to be part of a family like this!

They were open, too. Aileen had only just joined them and yet she was already accepted. He knew that if he and Rosalind were to— But that was something he had determined not even to think about. He wrote a letter to his hostess, Emily, thanking her sincerely for a wonderful evening.

When Rosalind phoned later that day he thought she might want to chat, but she was businesslike as well as friendly. She had phoned because he was on call.

'We've just admitted someone from A and E,' she said. 'It looks like peritonitis. Young lad, got stabbed in the abdomen a couple of nights ago. He decided to be tough, possibly because he knew the police were looking for him, so he tried to treat himself. I'm getting fluids into him but I haven't prescribed antibiotics yet. He's going to need surgery.'

'What are the symptoms?'

'He's lying on his back, knees up to his chest. Fast, shallow breathing, high temperature, small pulse. Abdomen is swollen and he's in considerable pain.'

'Sounds like we'd better open him up. I'll be over in five minutes. Want to assist?'

'I've just written to Emily,' he said to Rosalind as he stripped off his rubber gloves after he'd finished operating. 'I did enjoy myself last night. I wish I could cater like that. I'd have a dinner party every week.'

'You don't need to cook to have a dinner party,' she said. 'Why don't you have a sandwich party? You said yourself that you were a cordon bleu sandwich-maker.'

'Not little party sandwiches! I like big stuffed ones!'

'Then have a big stuffed, cordon bleu sandwich dinner party. People will love it. Not a cheese and wine, but a stuffed sandwich and wine party. I'll even come and act as your gracious hostess if you want.'

'I'd like that. But people would gossip.'

'Let them,' she said inelegantly.

She was baffling, Mark decided as he strolled back to Gingerbread Hall. She was other things, too—she was clever, hard-working, lovable and irritating in turn. And she was knock-down gorgeous. But mostly she was baffling.

She had spent that night with him and it had changed his life. He would have thought it would have changed hers, too, but there was no indication of it in her behaviour. Their amiable relationship seemed to be the same as ever. She'd even taken him to a family party as a friend.

He knew from the family, and from other people that he'd talked to, that she had the reputation of being tough and solitary. He'd seen another side to her—she could be hurt, could be afraid. But she hid it. Was she hiding something from him? He didn't know.

It would take a formidable younger man to be an equal for her.

He spent a restless afternoon and evening. There were things to do. Every Sunday he cleaned and tidied, keeping his little home immaculate. He liked it bare but exact. Then there were journals to read through, notes to check. He couldn't settle. He knew what it was, of course. He wanted to think about Rosalind. But he wouldn't—he couldn't. He'd made up his mind. So he worked even harder.

By early evening he was thoroughly dissatisfied. He wasn't sure what he wanted to do. He could go to the doctors' commonroom and chat to a colleague. He could go to the gym. Neither option really appealed to him. Then at eight there was a firm rap on the door.

He was surprised for not many people visited him here. There was a moment of excitement and anticipation—it might be Rosalind. Then his mouth twisted in disappointment as he remembered she had told him she was babysitting for Alex and Lisa.

On the doorstep was Aileen Wright.

Previously, he'd thought her entirely self-possessed. It was a feature she shared with Rosalind, though otherwise the two were different in character. But this evening she seemed uncertain, even embarrassed.

'Is it a good time to call?' she asked as he invited her in. 'Are you sure you're not just going out? Or working? I would have phoned but I didn't know your number.'

'Actually, I'd be glad of some company,' he said honestly. 'I've been too much on my own today, even though I was on the ward this morning.'

She looked thoughtful when he said this, and then

more relaxed. 'That makes my job easier. I don't like going behind people's backs, which I am doing.'

That surprised him. 'I wouldn't have thought that was like you,' he said, 'but sit on the couch and I'll make us some tea. This sounds serious.'

He wanted a minute to think. His heart was beating faster. It could only be Rosalind's back she was talking about. Aileen had been in the group when Rosalind had agreed to babysit tonight so she knew Rosalind couldn't be here.

He gave her tea and took his own to sit in his customary place with his back to the wall. 'I really enjoyed the party last night,' he offered.

She nodded. 'I thought you did, and so did I. It was a real family party. I'm hoping I'll be considered mother to three children, but I suspect I'll be of most use as a grandmother. Especially as two of the children are already happily married.'

She had regained her confidence now. When she looked at him in the calm way she had, he recognised the keen brain underneath. 'Which brings us to the unmarried Rosalind,' she said. 'What's wrong with her, Mark? I know it's something serious.'

The question left him speechless. How could she have known? He was a doctor, accustomed to keeping his thoughts, his suspicions, to himself. 'Is there anything wrong?' he tried to ask lightly.

It was no use. When he saw her half-smile he realised he hadn't fooled her. She'd noticed his initial shock. But he had to try. 'Being a houseman is a very stressful job,' he said. 'It takes it out of everybody.'

Aileen nodded. 'So I hear. And all the family have told me how tough and self-possessed Rosalind is. She's

even told me herself. She can cope with anything—if
there's a family problem Rosalind will come up with a
sensible answer even if it's a harsh one. We rely on her
to keep her head. The trouble is the family's got used to
this way of thinking. They don't see when things are
getting beyond even Rosalind.'

She paused. 'Go on,' Mark said. 'What you say
is…interesting.'

'I'm not a full family member yet so I can see things
from the outside. And looking at people—working out
what they're thinking—is my trade. There's something
badly wrong with Rosalind. And I've seen the way you
look at her when you think no one's looking at you.'

'What way's that?' he asked, trying to speak neutrally.

'First, and obviously, as if you're madly in love with
her. Second, as if you're terribly afraid. And, what is
worse, she's afraid and she's in love with you, too. Why
don't you admit it?'

'Me, afraid?' he asked, picking on just one thing.

'You are, aren't you?'

There didn't seem much point in denying it. She
wouldn't believe him if he did. 'You're a frightening
woman, Aileen. Am I as transparent as that?'

Aileen smiled. 'Let me boast a little—after all, it is
my job. And I'm still an outsider though I won't be for
much longer. I'm not just probing because I want to
know, Mark. I want to help.'

He sat there thinking, his eyes half-closed. He knew
she was watching him patiently, waiting for him to make
up his mind. The idea of telling someone else was suddenly very attractive. He realised what a burden the secret had been to him. What must it have been to
Rosalind?

'For a start, you can't help,' he said flatly. 'Nobody can help. I told her I'd tell anyone I felt ought to know so I'll tell you, as her nearly mother. There's no medical confidentiality involved. I'm not her doctor.'

There was no way to wrap things up prettily. 'Some weeks ago Rosalind was injected with blood from a patient with AIDS, Aileen. She could be infected. That would mean the end of her medical career and then death.'

Aileen was certainly tough herself. 'I see. When will you know for certain?'

'She's been having blood tests, but so far they're inconclusive. If there is no sign after three months then she's almost certainly free of infection.'

'That will be in...?'

'In a fortnight.'

'Right. Well, that answers one question. I take it nothing can be done?'

He shook his head. 'We treated her at once but, other than that, it's a case of wait and see. Probably the best thing for Rosalind is what she's doing now, what she's always done—working hard. She's one of the world's workers.'

He went on. 'But you're wrong about her being in love with me. She's desperately worried, even though she tries to pretend she's not. She just looks up to me because I'm trying to help her. She's got her life to come. I'm ten years older than her.'

'I'm thirteen years younger than her father, and yet neither of us has any hesitation in getting married.' She paused. 'Who're you trying to convince that she doesn't love you? Me or yourself?'

Mark winced. 'You don't pull your punches, do you,

Aileen? Still, it's a good question. I suppose I don't know my own feelings, I'm not a detached observer. I was married before. My first wife died of AIDS, caught in similar circumstances.'

He was glad Aileen maintained her dispassionate attitude. A clinical approach made things easier to bear. She said, 'It must make things very hard for you, knowing what Rosalind is going through. Don't you think she might really love you?'

'She might think she does. She might not in ten years time.'

'Do you love her?'

There was one obvious answer to that query. 'I won't allow myself to love her.'

Apparently, she had no more questions for him so he asked, 'Are you going to offer me any advice, Aileen?'

She shook her head. 'I wouldn't be so presumptuous. Perhaps I'd suggest that you could think again about things that you've already decided. It's hard to change your mind once it's made up. Being able to change your mind is sometimes a sign of strength, not weakness.' She looked down. 'D'you think I could have some more tea?'

'Of course! I'm sorry to be such a bad host.' It was when he stood to collect her cup that he saw the tear tracks on her cheeks. Now it was his turn to be understanding. 'These things hurt, don't they?' he asked gently.

She pulled out her handkerchief. 'It's part of being in the family. You have to suffer as well as enjoy. I hope you don't think I'm an interfering old woman?'

'No, I'm glad you came. And I think John is a very lucky man.' He kissed her gently on the cheek.

He felt calmer when Aileen had gone. She was right. It *was* hard to change your mind. But talking to Aileen had crystallised his ideas and made him more certain of what he wanted—as well as more certain of what he could not have.

Now he knew he loved Rosalind and he wanted to marry her. He couldn't imagine anyone else making him so happy. When she had shared his bed he had been transported. Together they'd found something that previously he'd only dreamed of.

But she meant more to him than that. He liked talking to her, liked the way she laughed at his jokes—they were in tune. And Aileen was right. Ten years was not too much. He knew of happy marriages with a larger gap between the partners.

So why didn't he ask her to marry him? He suspected she'd say yes. That was the problem. First, he was older than her and her boss—he knew only too well it was easier to be seduced by academic prowess than it was by money or good looks. Second, she was under such great strain. Even though she thought she knew what she was doing, it was possible she didn't.

He wondered. As he tried desperately to be cool, analytical and thoughtful he remembered her face and her body, and emotion took over.

Rosalind liked babysitting Holly and Jack—they were good company. They'd insisted on helping her to cook the tea, and afterwards they'd all played Scrabble before the two went to bed.

She wondered if she was missing something. How had her two career-minded sisters entered domesticity so readily? Perhaps it was restricting but it was so comforting. She deliberately didn't think about what it entailed—a man to marry.

When Lisa and Alex came back she refused their offer of a bed for the night and said she wanted to be ready on the job the next day. This wasn't really the reason. She just wanted to be alone with her rather depressing thoughts and the company of a happily married couple wasn't going to help her. Alex ordered her a taxi to go back to the hospital.

Just after midnight she was sitting on her bed when there was a loud bang on her door. She frowned. It was strange. People in the residency tended to respect sleep times.

She opened the door to Alison. 'Wanna come in,' Alison said in a slurred voice. 'Wanna drink with my pal.'

She was dressed in dark trousers and what once had been a smart silk blouse. But there were stains on the blouse, her make-up was smudged and her hair looked a mess. Alison looked drunk, but not very happy about it.

'Come in,' said Rosalind. Ordinarily she would have had little time for friends who drank too much and then came looking for sympathy, but there was an expression on Alison's face that worried her. She looked afraid. Her eyes had the hunted look of an animal that realises there's nothing it can do about approaching danger.

Alison lurched in and slumped unsteadily on the bed. She drank from a wine bottle she held in her hand. Rosalind hadn't noticed it before. She looked at her friend in horror. This wasn't the Alison she knew!

'Have some…some wine,' Alison mumbled, waving the bottle vaguely in Rosalind's direction. Rosalind grabbed it to stop it spilling. 'Have you been celebrating something?' Rosalind asked. 'Or was this just a party?'

Alison answered by bursting into tears. 'Went to see Harold,' she wailed, then there were no more answers. Her body jerked as she sobbed.

Rosalind looked at her friend speculatively. She hadn't seen much of her recently. On the few occasions they had spoken Alison had appeared to be slightly depressed, but managing to cope with the pressure of work. When questioned, she hadn't been taking the same joy in it that Rosalind was. 'I suppose I'm managing,' she had said, and had fended off further questions.

Rosalind had seen and dealt with drunks before. She took Alison's shoulders and shook her. 'What happened when you went to see Harold?' she asked sharply. 'Did you have another argument?'

'I've had enough. Just had enough. N-no argument with Harold. I went round to see him 'cos I wanted him back. I found him with this girl—they're living together. Well, that's all right, I suppose. But it turns out he's been seeing her for years. When he had to choose between us he chose her. Kept us both going together. I could have been looking round. I used to get lots of invitations. But not now…'

Alison's voice tapered off and her eyelids closed. 'Wish my ears would stop ringing,' she muttered. 'Shouldn't have taken those pills…'

Rosalind was instantly alert.

'What pills, Alison?' she snapped. But Alison merely sagged against the wall. Rosalind grabbed her tightly by the hair, pulled her face forward and slapped it hard. 'I said, "What pills, Alison?"'

Alison opened her eyes in shock and tried to focus.

'Hurt,' she groaned. 'And my ears hurt. What pills? Just aspirin, Ros'lin', just aspirin.'

Rosalind gritted her teeth and slapped Alison again. 'How many aspirin?'

'Few in a plastic strip. Found them in my cupboard.' She sobbed. 'What have I done, Rosalind? I feel such a fool. And my stomach aches. I didn't want to do it, Rosalind, I didn't want to do it and I feel such a fool.' Alison's eyes shut again.

Rosalind rushed down to Alison's room. The door was open and the light on. On the floor was a plastic container, which had held twelve aspirins. Quickly she looked around the rest of the room. She knew that would-be suicides didn't usually hide the evidence of what they'd taken. There were no more bottles, strips or anything. Closing the door, she went back to her own room.

Alison was stretched on her bed. She was sweating and breathing too heavily.

Rosalind knew what she should do. A quick call and Alison would be transported to the A and E department, her stomach washed out with an alkaline solution and a litre of five per cent sodium bicarbonate left in. She'd recover.

But A and E departments notoriously hated suicides, real or attention-seeking. And there was no way a junior doctor's suicide attempt could be kept quiet. It was vastly different from her own accident. Hospital gossips would have a field day. Alison's career would be ruined. The attempt would be reported to the GMC, who would probably suspend her. For a moment Rosalind paused. This was a decision she just didn't want to make. She lifted the phone and dialled Mark's number.

A drowsy voice said, 'I'm not on call. This had better be important.'

'Mark, this is Rosalind. I'm in the residency. Alison is here in my room. She's taken an overdose. Aspirin, I'm pretty certain.'

He was awake at once, aware of the problems and realising why she had phoned him. 'You don't want to take her to A and E. You're sure it's not necessary?'

She was dicing with her friend's life and her reputation. 'I don't think it's necessary. Not yet.'

'Get her awake. I'll pick you both up in five minutes.' He rang off.

Somehow Rosalind managed to get Alison awake. There was no coherent speech, but at least her eyes were open and she'd stand with support. Rosalind managed to walk her up and down the little room.

Mark arrived, pushing open her door without knocking. He was in jeans, T-shirt and trainers but no socks. His face was grim. Quickly he examined Alison—taking her pulse, checking her breathing, looking at her eyes.

'Back to Gingerbread Hall?' he asked Rosalind.

She hesitated. Alison was her friend, not his. 'If you don't mind,' she said. 'I think I'm pushing my problems onto you.'

'You are. I hope Alison realises what a friend she's got.' Then he did something that surprised her. He leaned over and quickly kissed her on the forehead. 'She's lucky,' he said.

Alison could walk, almost. Luck was with them. Rosalind checked that no one was around, and Mark half helped, half carried Alison down to his car. When they arrived at Gingerbread Hall he carried her upstairs to the bathroom. Rosalind noticed the easy way he carried her friend upstairs. He was strong.

Alison was half-awake but queasy when they got her to the bathroom. 'You know what we have to do now?' Mark asked.

Rosalind sighed. 'She's got to be sick. Come on, let's get on with it.'

It wasn't the most romantic way of spending time with him, but a lot of medicine wasn't romantic. Mark had a skill, she'd noticed, of making the most unpleasant physical action into something that the patient could endure with some dignity. It was a skill more often found in nurses than doctors, and it was something she envied.

Eventually Mark decided that probably the best thing for Alison was to try to sleep things off. She'd been sick, and had managed to drink some water. He washed her face and carried her to his bedroom.

'Not as much fun as the last time we were in here together,' he said to Rosalind.

She patted him affectionately. 'You said that to embarrass me,' she said, 'and I'm duly embarrassed.' He left her to undress her friend.

She wasn't embarrassed. She was aware of what he'd done—how he'd lightened the mood, stopped her from being feeling too indebted to him. He was a man of infinite subtlety.

'We'd better keep an eye on her through the night,' he said when she came downstairs. 'We'll take it in turns to doze by her bedside. If she wakes try to get her to drink some more water. She'll be dehydrated.'

'No. She's my friend, and I've lumbered you with something you could have done without, I've even turned you out of your bed. I'll look after her.'

'This is my house, young Grey. I've made a medical decision about Alison, and I'm going to share the consequences. Anyway, she should be all right for half an hour now. Would you like a drink of any sort?'

The question surprised her. Then she realised that she did want something but she didn't know what. 'I'm not going to sleep yet. And I would like a drink—anything but alcohol.'

He grinned. 'After seeing what it did to Alison I know what you mean. We'll have a cup of Earl Grey tea each. Now, I know it's got unfortunate recent memories, but if you go up and have a shower in my bathroom you'll feel better.'

'I'd like that.' She sniffed. 'But my clothes smell a bit.'

'I've got a dressing-gown you can borrow.' His face remained polite but she knew he was teasing her.

'Borrow it again?' she asked with a grin. 'Well, I suppose circumstances are different. You said I could take it home but I seem to use it more here.'

She did feel better after a shower. She came down and sat in her usual place on the couch and he fetched her some tea. 'Would you like to listen to some music?' he asked. 'Something calming, perhaps?'

She was curious. 'You've never played music while I've been here before. I didn't know you liked it.'

'I don't like background music. When you've been here in the past I've wanted to talk and to listen to you. But now would be a good time to listen properly.' He moved over to his stereo and soon the room was filled with the sound of a piano.

She did as he'd suggested and listened properly. The music slowly took hold of her, moved her, suggested there was love and hope in the world, then calmed her. After twenty minutes it finished.

'That was good for me,' she told him. 'How d'you know what things will move me and how I feel?'

'I just pick the things I like best. We must be alike.'

She thought about this.

'We need to think about Alison,' he said. 'We've taken her out of the medical system by bringing her here. Now she's our responsibility, and we have to decide about what to do next. D'you know what brought this on?'

'Man trouble,' Rosalind said laconically. She told him about Alison's trip to see Harold again. 'She also told me about her attempt to seduce you,' she went on. 'Mark, a lot of men would have taken advantage of that kind of offer.'

He shrugged, obviously embarrassed. 'She's just a kid, Rosalind. We have nothing in common.'

'She's my age,' Rosalind pointed out impishly.

'No, she's not. She'll still be half a kid when she's fifty. You know more about life now than she will then.'

'Will she be a good doctor?'

He looked thoughtful. 'I think she will. She won't be a surgeon, but the basic competence is there and a great deal of thoughtfulness. She will be a good doctor, but she can't carry on as she has done tonight. It's such a waste!'

'I don't think she'll do anything like this again. I think she's learned her lesson.' He looked at her expressionlessly. 'This is a hard decision to take, Rosalind. You're suggesting we just forget the whole thing—not insist she have counselling or see a psychologist? She's only twenty-four. Perhaps we should contact her parents.'

'She won't do it again. This was a one-off occurrence.'

'How can you be so sure?'

'Because when she realised what she'd done she felt stupid. She so obviously wanted a second chance. I've known her for years and basically she's a hard-working, down-to-earth girl.'

Rosalind saw him thinking, considering what she had said. He wasn't going to just accept her decision, but had to make up his own mind. She rather liked that.

'All right,' he said, 'but I'll want to talk to her myself.'

'You've got to work together. You'll have to get things sorted first.' Rosalind yawned. 'Where are you going to sleep?' she asked.

'You're going to sleep on that couch, with a pillow and a duvet. I'll catnap in a chair by the bed.'

'No. I won't have it. This is my case, Doctor. I'll catnap upstairs.'

He recognised her determination. 'We'll compromise. You can do the first three hours then I'll take over,' he said. 'You'll be no good on the ward tomorrow if you have no sleep.'

She accepted that—it made sense.

She knew he must be tired but he made no move to usher her upstairs. He was looking at her with unusual intensity. 'Rosalind...' he started, then fell silent again. It seemed as if he was trying to find the right words to say to her.

Eventually, he said, 'Rosalind, have you ever felt an emotion so strong that you had to act on it, even though you knew your actions might be wrong?'

She knew he wasn't talking about Alison. She also

knew that, although the question had been asked casually, the answer would be vastly important to him. She had to get the answer right.

First she thought. Then, choosing her words carefully, she said, 'I've always been proud of my brain, my reasoning powers. I've always been proud of acting logically, not being swayed by emotion. I've tended to distrust people who put emotion first. Now I'm wondering if I've been right all the time. I suspect that what I feel is right is likely to be just as true as what I think is right.'

Was that the right answer? she asked herself.

He didn't comment on it. 'Up to the bedroom, Rosalind. We'll both need what sleep we can get. I'll relieve you in three hours.'

She stood and kissed him briefly on the forehead. 'Thank for what you've done,' she said, and skipped upstairs.

Alison seemed to be all right. Rosalind settled herself in a chair and wrapped a blanket round herself. She could doze.

She wondered what exactly had been the point of Mark's question.

CHAPTER TEN

ROSALIND was still asleep on Mark's couch when he brought Alison down next morning. They'd changed places in the middle of the night. She had snuggled under his duvet, still warm from his body, but it hadn't stopped her sleeping.

'I'll get you two ladies some breakfast,' Mark said urbanely. 'Alison, why don't you sit by Rosalind a while?'

Alison looked decidedly woebegone. Last night Rosalind had managed to get her into a pair of Mark's pyjamas. This morning Mark had given her a blanket to wrap round herself. She shuffled over to the couch, and Rosalind sat up to give her some room. She put her arm round her. 'How d'you feel, love?' she asked.

The tears started flowing. 'I feel physically wrecked and stupid and guilty. How could I do such a thing? And you brought me here! I don't deserve friends like you.'

'Perhaps you'll do the same for me one day,' Rosalind said, hoping fervently that she'd never have to do any such thing.

Alison obviously felt the same way. 'I don't think that's very likely. God, I never knew that doing things like this was so unpleasant. I won't do it again.'

'I'm sure you won't, ' Rosalind said drily.

After a while Mark called them over to breakfast. It was simple—cereals, toast, fruit juice and coffee. 'I don't think I can eat anything,' Alison said.

'Try,' Mark urged her. 'You need something in your stomach. Apart from anything else, you need the energy.' So Alison tried to eat, and when she'd nibbled on some dry toast and drunk some milky coffee she said she felt better.

'I did finish up in your bed eventually,' she said to Mark with a faint grin, 'even if it wasn't the way I'd intended to.'

He looked at her judiciously. 'I think you're improving,' he said. 'Now, you're to take the day off—phone in sick. You can stay here, if you want, or go back to your own room.'

'I don't feel sick—' she started, but he interrupted her.

'Just do what the doctor orders. You need the time off. When you're feeling better I want a long talk with you so get your strength up. Now, here or back to the residency?'

She decided to go back to her room, but declined the offer of a lift. 'What are you going to wear?' Rosalind asked blandly.

Alison flinched. 'I'm going to bin those clothes anyway,' she said, 'and they're too much of a mess to put on now.'

'I'll fetch you something,' Rosalind offered, and set off at once. When she returned Alison was having a bath.

'She's resilient,' Mark said. 'With any luck, she'll put all this behind her. It might even make her a better doctor.' He smiled at Rosalind. 'We didn't follow the proper medical procedure, did we? How d'you feel about it?'

'All right,' she said, 'I know what you're going to say. Medicine is an art as well as a science.'

'There is an autumnal sun outside,' Mark said to Rosalind a week later. 'At lunchtime we will walk in the grounds, two colleagues strolling in a leisurely fashion discussing matters of medical importance.'

She rose from the desk at which she'd been working, groaned and stretched. 'Anything to get me away from this paperwork. But you normally work through your lunchbreak.'

'I just feel like playing hookey,' he said. 'Set off at one?'

'Downstairs in the foyer. I'll need to change my shoes.'

The weather was getting cooler now, and she was glad of her coat. He led her through the grounds of the hospital, away from the main blocks to where there was grass, undergrowth and even a few great trees.

They sat together on a fallen log. The buildings were out of sight, and they could have been in the middle of the country. There were even birds calling in the branches above them.

Mark had chatted amiably about nothing in particular, and Rosalind had tried to respond to his mood. But it hadn't worked. 'I know you too well now,' she accused him as they sat side by side. 'You're not really happy, it's all a bit strained. Tell me what you really want to say.'

He looked at her quizzically. 'And I thought I was fooling you. D'you know everything I'm thinking, Rosalind? Actually, I was going to suggest that you give up medicine and take up police work. No one could lie to you.'

'Come on,' she said impatiently. 'It must be important for you to drag me away from the ward.'

'It is. I want to talk about your next test.'

If he hadn't mentioned it she could have kept it in the back of her mind. It was always there, of course. Every morning she knew she was a day nearer knowing her fate, but it helped not to have to talk about it.

'What about it?' she asked, dry-mouthed.

'I'll take the blood tomorrow and we'll get the results on Saturday morning. This is the important one. You've shown no signs of infection so far, but that's to be expected. If you're free of infection on Saturday then we can take it you're free for good. We'll test again after six months, but it's not really necessary.'

'I know,' she said. 'I think I know everything about the test.'

'I want to take the blood myself,' he went on, 'and, of course, whatever the result I'll ask for a retest.'

'Fair enough. I want to be with you when you pick up the results.'

He looked at her, surprised. 'I'm not sure that's a good idea. You should be nearby, of course, but not at the lab. I'll—'

'It's my life you're handling, I want to be there.'

He saw she was serious. 'If that's what you want.'

'Of course,' he went on, 'if you are HIV positive that's not the end of the world. There are new drugs coming on line every day and the research that is going on is bound to throw something up soon. Many people who are positive live for years—'

She stopped him. 'Please, Mark, don't bother. I've heard it all, I know it all. There isn't an article, a textbook, available I haven't read through, looking for a loophole. I know the odds. And don't try to give me the usual bromide about living a reasonable life when I'm positive. I once heard an orthopaedic consultant talking to a climber who had fallen and broken his back. He'd never walk again. The consultant was telling him that the latest wheelchairs were very mobile. Some consolation!'

She knew her voice was getting shrill. She was screaming at Mark because he was the only target available. He put his arm round her shoulders and pulled her to him. She hadn't known how comforting simple closeness could be.

She forced her voice to normality and eased herself out of his embrace. She wiped her face and blew her nose. She was Dr Rosalind Grey—she could cope!

'Sorry,' she said. 'I won't disgrace myself again. I know these things happen, it's just unfortunate. I can take it.'

He said, 'I can't know how you feel, I can only guess, but I'm going to do something terrible. I'm going to make you feel worse.'

'Can you?' she asked with a half-smile.

'Yes, with four words. What about your family?'

She hadn't known he could be so cruel, but she realised it was something else she'd pushed to the back of her mind. She knew only too well what effect the news would have on her sisters, their families, her father and now Aileen.

'I don't have to tell them at once,' she said.

'You do. If you don't I will.'

She knew he meant it. 'They'll be heart-broken,' she said. 'We've been so close since—since my mother went.'

'You're going to have to tell them,' Mark said, 'whatever the result.'

'I know.'

'And what about your friends?' Mark asked. 'What about me?'

'You've made me cry again,' she whispered. 'Mark, I'm frightened.'

'So am I,' he muttered.

It was a curious, unexpected skill Rosalind discovered she had. Part of the houseman's job was dealing with much of the reams of paperwork that flooded onto the ward. Everyone hated it. Reports were lost, doctors forgot to sign requisitions, nurses didn't fill in all their obs. But Rosalind could organise it. The ward paperwork now flowed in and flowed out, organised and policed by her. 'Would you like a job as a ward clerk?' the sister asked. 'We'd even pay your wages out of our own pockets.'

It was Friday afternoon, the Friday before the Saturday on which she would get her results. She sat in the doctors' room, surveying the completed and neatly arranged piles of paper, mildly pleased with herself.

'Busy?' Mark asked as when entered.

She waved at the papers. 'It's called displacement activity. I fill my life with little things so I don't have to worry about the big things.'

'Paperwork is not a little thing,' he corrected her. 'We once had a primary school teacher in here, and for some reason I asked her what the first thing was she had to do if there was a fire.'

'Save the registers,' Rosalind guessed. 'I suppose it makes sense.'

He looked hurt. 'You always spoil my stories, young Grey. Too clever for your own good. Now, I'd particularly like you to come to dinner tonight. Have you any plans?'

She hadn't, and the prospect of an evening with Mark was a good one. 'No, I'd love to come to dinner. What kind of sandwiches tonight?'

'Aha! I have a secret ingredient. These will be sandwiches such as you've never tasted.'

'Oysters?' she guessed cheekily.

'Oysters, indeed! No, something else special. About half past seven?'

'Looking forward to it.'

Rosalind dressed carefully before she walked over to Gingerbread Hall. Her blouse was of white silk, and she wore it with a long skirt in a deep emerald green. She knew it was conventional for redheads to wear green, but it suited her and she liked the way it swished round her legs. For a moment she thought of buying a bottle of wine to take, but she thought that after last time it might be taken as a hint.

After tomorrow she'd never walk towards Mark's home again in the same way. She knew they'd still be friends but their relationship had been coloured by the fact that she might have contracted HIV. She must remind him of Frances, his ex-wife. How would he feel if she was free of the virus? Pleased for her, of course, but there would be no need to feel sorry for her, no need to protect her.

She wondered if she'd ever find another man like him. Certainly he was older, but so what? Both her sisters had married older men, and her father was about to marry a younger woman. She loved Mark. Of that she was sure. What she did not know was how he felt about her. She thought that he loved her, but had decided he was not the right man for her. He ought to let me be the judge of that, she thought morosely.

She knocked on the door and Mark opened it. 'You look gorgeous,' he said, obviously impressed by her dress. 'Do come in.' She didn't at first, but looked at him thoughtfully. Instead of his customary casual dress he, too, was dressed smartly in a sea-island cotton shirt as white as her own blouse, a rich blue silk tie and black trousers, expensively cut.

'Why are you dressed like that?' she asked.

He pulled her inside. 'I might ask you the same question but I will only say that it proves we are soul-mates. We think the same things, feel the same way, and tonight is a night to celebrate.'

There was a further shock as she stepped inside. She sniffed. 'If I didn't know you better I'd say you'd been cooking,' she told him, 'and cooking expertly, too.'

'Surprise time,' he said. 'This evening things are going to be different.'

They certainly were. Two chairs were drawn up to a white-clothed table, and there were shining glasses and silver. With a flourish he lit two candles.

'We had candles on the island,' she said.

'Another happy memory. In fact, I wondered if having candles wasn't going too far, but I was persuaded and now I'm glad.'

She was still bewildered. 'But we always have sandwiches.'

'First there's my little joke. Today we start with oysters au gratin. Then we have smoked salmon. Main course is duck in Pernod sauce, with wild rice and fresh vegetables. Ice cream, fruit salad and cheese to end with.'

'You didn't cook all that?' she asked incredulously.

He shook his head. 'I did intend to persuade you that I had, but in fact I got a little firm of cooks to come in and do it for me. They've just left—been driving me distracted all afternoon.'

'Why did you do all this?'

'Because I wanted to give you a good meal. And I didn't want to take you out—I wanted it to be just us together.'

'A bit like Wellington's ball before Waterloo,' she mumbled.

'A very apt comparison. Remember, we won at Waterloo. Now, shall we start with champagne?' There was a satisfying pop as he pulled a cork.

It was a wonderful meal, and to Rosalind's surprise it did take her mind off things. They ate slowly, enjoying everything.

'I've spent too much time lately regarding food as just fuel,' she said, 'to be eaten quickly so I could get on with my work.'

'A common fault. I do the same. Mind you, I wouldn't want to dine like this every night. The sandwich has its place.'

Finally there was coffee, which they had in front of the fire, and a silver plate with a handful of petits fours. 'Just to tempt the palate,' he said. She didn't think it was possible to eat anything more but somehow she managed to eat two, and they were delicious.

'One left,' he said, pushing it to the centre of the plate.

She sighed. 'I couldn't. I've eaten just enough and I feel marvellous.'

'I think you'll especially enjoy this last one.'

Some tone in his voice made her look at him. She took the little scrap of frilly paper and opened it. It wasn't a confection of cream or caramel. It was a ring. A gold band with a solitaire emerald. 'What's this?' she whispered.

'It's an engagement ring.'

For a few moments she stared at the ring, as if hypnotised, then she looked up at him, her expression haunted.

'I want you to marry me, Rosalind,' he said.

She was bewildered. Nothing had led her to expect this. She said the first thing that came into her head. 'Wait till tomorrow when I get the results.'

'No!' He was vehement. 'We must decide tonight.'

'But tomorrow we'll know if—'

'That's why we must decide tonight. I'm not asking you because I feel sorry for you. I love you, whether you're ill or not. I think I've loved you ever since you appeared at my bedside on the island.'

She took the ring, looking at the richness of the green gleam in the emerald. Offering it to him, she spread out her hand. 'Put it on my finger,' she said.

Silently, he did so. 'And I've always loved you,' she said. 'Of course I'll marry you.'

He kissed her, a kiss that fused all her hopes, all her dreams, into one incandescent joy. He loved her—they were going to get married!

Breaking away from him, she rose. 'We're an old engaged couple now, Mark,' she said. 'Why don't you take me to bed?'

She awoke early, smiling, in his bed. Her night had been ecstatic—she thought their love had reached new bounds, gone beyond what previously she had thought were the limits of joy.

'Do you want some coffee?' she asked.

'I want you. Coffee after.' His arms closed round her again.

Eventually they had to get up, and this time she did make the coffee. 'I'm going to learn all sorts of domestic skills,' she said. 'Sewing and cleaning and cooking.'

'I'll teach you to make sandwiches,' he offered.

'Thank you. A necessary beginning to married life.' She frowned. 'Mark, can I phone my sisters and father and tell them we're engaged? They'll probably want us to come round tonight.'

'I have a confession to make. I really want to marry you so I can be part of your family. I'm not going to be a family friend any more. I'm going to be a real, proper family member, and that thought makes me very happy.'

She leaned over to kiss him. 'I think there's just a bit of truth there. And I love you more because you love them.'

'So phone away,' he said.

'I thought so,' said Lisa.

'About time,' said Emily.

Her father wasn't in, but Aileen said she was happy for them and thought they were both very lucky.

Then their mood calmed a little. She was still deliriously happy but there was business to be done.

'I'll go to the residency and change,' she said, 'then I'll meet you at the lab.'

She could tell that this was harder on him than it was on her. His face was stricken. 'It doesn't matter, Mark,' she said, putting her arms around him. 'I've got you, we've got each other. Whatever happens now, our life will be happy.'

'In the lab in twenty minutes,' he said hoarsely.

They stood unselfconsciously in the corridor, hand in hand. Her hand was uppermost. She looked down frequently to see the slim gold band and the gleaming emerald. It made her happy.

'Dr Harrison?' A white-coated technician came out, an envelope in her hand. 'This is for you.'

Rosalind shut her eyes. He took away his hand. She registered the sound of the envelope tearing, the crackle of the paper.

'Guess what, young Grey,' an amused voice said. 'You're healthy...'

MILLS & BOON®

Medical Romance™

COMING NEXT MONTH

'Twas The Night Before Christmas...

CAROL'S CHRISTMAS by Margaret Barker

Carol needed to talk to her husband, Euan, the new Casualty consultant. Did he *really* want the divorce to go through?

INSTANT FATHER CHRISTMAS by Josie Metcalfe

Midwife Livvy was so busy, she missed the signs of her own labour! Perhaps it had something to do with the unexpected arrival of her estranged husband, Daniel.

ONE MAGICAL KISS by Helen Shelton

Will persuaded Maggie to give him just one Christmas Eve kiss to put an end to his attempts to seduce her. But what a kiss!

MIRACLES AND MARRIAGE by Meredith Webber

Emma was wary. It was hard to take Patrick seriously in his Father Christmas outfit but when he kept mentioning marriage, it was even harder.

CHRISTMAS

Affairs

MORE THAN JUST KISSES UNDER THE MISTLETOE...

Enjoy three sparkling seasonal romances by your
favourite authors from

MILLS & BOON®
Presents™

HELEN BIANCHIN
For Anique, the season of goodwill has become...
The Seduction Season

SANDRA MARTON
Can Santa weave a spot of Christmas magic for Nick
and Holly in... *A Miracle on Christmas Eve?*

SHARON KENDRICK
Will Aleck and Clemmie have a... *Yuletide Reunion?*

MILLS & BOON®

Makes any time special™

Available from 6th November 1998

MILLS & BOON®

Next Month's Romance Titles

♡

Each month you can choose from a wide variety of romance novels from Mills & Boon®. Below are the new titles to look out for next month from the Presents™ and Enchanted™ series.

Presents™

PACIFIC HEAT	Anne Mather
THE BRIDAL BED	Helen Bianchin
THE YULETIDE CHILD	Charlotte Lamb
MISTLETOE MISTRESS	Helen Brooks
A CHRISTMAS SEDUCTION	Amanda Browning
THE THIRTY-DAY SEDUCTION	Kay Thorpe
FIANCÉE BY MISTAKE	Kate Walker
A NICE GIRL LIKE YOU	Alexandra Sellers

Enchanted™

FIANCÉ FOR CHRISTMAS	Catherine George
THE HUSBAND PROJECT	Leigh Michaels
COMING HOME FOR CHRISTMAS	Laura Martin
THE BACHELOR AND THE BABIES	Heather MacAllister
THE NUTCRACKER PRINCE	Rebecca Winters
FATHER BY MARRIAGE	Suzanne Carey
THE BILLIONAIRE'S BABY CHASE	Valerie Parv
ROMANTICS ANONYMOUS	Lauryn Chandler

On sale from 4th December 1998

H1 9811

Available at most branches of WH Smith, Tesco, Asda, Martins, Borders and all good paperback bookshops

Your Special Christmas Gift

Three romance novels from Mills & Boon® to
unwind with at your leisure—
and a luxurious Le Jardin bath gelée to pamper
you and gently wash your cares away.

for just £5.99

Featuring
Carole Mortimer—Married by Christmas
Betty Neels—A Winter Love Story
Jo Leigh—One Wicked Night

MILLS & BOON®

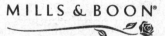

Makes your Christmas time special

Available from 23rd October 1998

4 FREE

books and a surprise gift!

We would like to take this opportunity to thank you for reading this Mills & Boon® book by offering you the chance to take FOUR more specially selected titles from the Medical Romance™ series absolutely FREE! We're also making this offer to introduce you to the benefits of the Reader Service™—

- ★ FREE home delivery
- ★ FREE gifts and competitions
- ★ FREE monthly Newsletter
- ★ Books available before they're in the shops
- ★ Exclusive Reader Service discounts

Accepting these FREE books and gift places you under no obligation to buy, you may cancel at any time, even after receiving your free shipment. Simply complete your details below and return the entire page to the address below. *You don't even need a stamp!*

YES! Please send me 4 free Medical Romance books and a surprise gift. I understand that unless you hear from me, I will receive 4 superb new titles every month for just £2.30 each, postage and packing free. I am under no obligation to purchase any books and may cancel my subscription at any time. The free books and gift will be mine to keep in any case.

M8YE

Ms/Mrs/Miss/Mr..................................Initials ....
BLOCK CAPITALS PLEASE

Surname ....

Address ....

....

....Postcode..................................

Send this whole page to:
The Reader Service, Freepost, Croydon, CR9 3WZ
(Eire readers please send coupon to: P.O. Box 4546, Dublin 24.)

Offer not valid to current Reader Service subscribers to this series. We reserve the right to refuse an application and applicants must be aged 18 years or over. Only one application per household. Terms and prices subject to change without notice. Offer expires 31st May 1999. As a result of this application, you may receive further offers from Harlequin Mills & Boon and other carefully selected companies. If you would prefer not to share in this opportunity please write to The Data Manager, P.O. Box 236, Croydon, Surrey CR9 3RU.

Medical Romance is being used as a trademark.

MILLS & BOON®

*M*akes
any time
special

Enjoy a romantic novel from
Mills & Boon®

Presents™ *Enchanted*™ *Temptation*

Historical Romance™ *Medical Romance*™